DARK MINDS

An Anthology of Dark Fiction

DARK MINDS

An Anthology of Dark Fiction

Published by

Dark Minds Press

31 Gristmill Close

Cheltenham

Glos.

GL51 0PZ

www.darkmindspress.com

Mail@darkmindspress.com

ISBN: 978-0-9566580-0-5

This Paperback First Edition 2011

Cover Image © Vincent Chong

Interior Artwork © Will Jaques

Selected and Prepared for Publication by Ross Warren

Printed and Bound in the UK by MPG Group King's Lynn and Bodmin

TABLE OF CONTENTS

The Ghost of Rain

Gary McMahon

i. the Website

It was Kayla's idea, and at first he wondered why on earth he hadn't thought of it himself. It was one of those suggestions that can only be made by someone who knows you as well – or even better – than you know yourself, someone who has spent a lot of time soaking up your wants and needs, your likes and dislikes.

"Why don't you see if you can find a recording of the rain? That might help." She had said it late one Sunday evening, when Frank was preparing for another sleepless night before going back to work on Monday morning. It was an off-hand thing; she was making tomorrow's sandwiches as she threw the words over her shoulder, not really thinking about what she was saying or where they might land.

"You what?" He put down his book (a collection of WWI poetry, lent to him by Maria, a colleague at the office) and glanced at her over his glasses. She loved it when he did that; she said it made him look 'professor-sexy'. At least, that's what she *used* to say, before things got so fraught between them.

"You know," she said, wrapping the thin sandwiches in sheets of tinfoil. "To help you sleep." She was biting her lip, concentrating. She didn't want to use too much of the tinfoil – it was expensive, and things were getting tight.

"Why the hell didn't I think of it? Great idea...only, where do you think I'd get hold of something like that?" He stood, walked over to the television and turned down the volume. "I mean, who would sell a recording of the rain?"

Kayla came through into the lounge, rubbing her hands on her jeans. Her hair was coming loose from the Alice band and she was squinting in one eye, trying to readjust the dangling strands of her fringe by force of will alone. It needed dyeing again; the dark roots were showing through. "I dunno. Try the web. There are probably loads of websites dedicated to that stuff. I bet you can download MP3s of whatever you want. I read in a magazine the other week that someone's set up a business offering digital recordings of their own orgasms. How gross is that?" Her eyes flashed, as if she didn't find it gross at all, but instead found it rather stimulating.

Frank turned to her, shaking his head. "Christ, what a world." He shook his head again, half smiling yet secretly shocked that someone would do such a thing, sell such an intimate moment of their lives.

"Yep. Everyone's got an angle these days." Kayla sat down and picked up the newspaper, looking through the TV listings, planning her evening's viewing. She looked small and too thin, as if the sofa were swallowing her up.

The Ghost of Rain

Frank had suffered from insomnia for most of his life, but the strength and frequency of these bouts differed each time it happened.

This time, he knew, it was a result of the financial situation in which they'd found themselves. He couldn't deny that the threat of redundancy and the rapidly shrinking job market were causing him to lose sleep. The reason was obvious; it was the cure that remained elusive.

He went upstairs, into the study (which was actually the third bedroom of their 1960s semi detached home in a suburb of Leeds) and booted up the laptop. It took a while for the machine to come to life – it really needed looking at, but they didn't have the money to spare. He stared at the screen, willing it to flicker and show him the start-up page, and as he did so he remembered when he was a boy, and the way that the sound of rain falling against the windows of the family home would always lull him into a long, deep sleep.

Frank's childhood had been tough. His father was an alcoholic and his parents had argued what seemed like all the time, but the sanctuary of his little room, especially when it was raining (and didn't it always seem to be raining in Yorkshire in the 1970s?) had always offered him a safe place to hide from the storm.

Finally the screen flared up, chugging through to the main page where he typed in his log-in details and waited for the operating system to kick into gear.

Once he was able, Frank brought up his internet explorer and went to a search engine, then typed in the words "recording of rainfall" and watched the screen bring forth a series of matches to his keywords.

At first the results were disappointing. Whichever link he clicked with the cursor led him down an electronic blind alley. There were countless hits on the words 'rain' and 'recording', but none of them provided what he actually needed – a digital recording of rainfall. Then, via a series of chat rooms and secondary links, he stumbled upon the webpage of a company called Soundlings.com.

The page itself was rather cheap-looking, with ugly font and clumsy hyperlinks to samples of various weird and not-so-wonderful recordings. At a glance, Frank discovered that, if he were so inclined, he could download the sound of a cat being run over, a dog getting shot with a small calibre revolver, a body falling from a bridge, and a handful of other equally disturbing sounds.

Then, thankfully, his cursor hovered over and highlighted something much more promising. The link promised "sounds of nature", and the accompanying blurb mentioned thunderstorms, windstorms, and rainsfall (sic).

Frank clicked on the link, waited for the page to refresh and a connection to be made, and then scanned the list which appeared before him, hoping that his search would soon be over.

The list began quite simply, with titles like "bumble bees", "birdsong" and "grass cutting", but things soon degenerated into something darker. He refused to even think about what he might hear if he listened to "murdergirl" or "raper" or "cuttinghim".

He was just about to close down the browser when he caught sight of something that drew his attention. There was a second list, this one running down the right hand side of the screen, and among these less horrifying titles was one named "rainsong".

Frank felt his shoulders relax. He hadn't even been aware that they were tense, but the muscles had bunched up and his posture had slipped into a hunched position.

Each sound file offered a clip, a small snatch of what was contained in the full download. Frank clicked the title, and when a dialogue box appeared asking if he wanted to sample or save the entire file, he chose the former, unable to ignore the slight hint of apprehension which accompanied the action.

There was a short moment of silence, and then his computer speakers began to omit a sound. Gentle at first, but building in volume, there came the familiar sound of rainfall. But it was not simply rain falling; it was the exact sound that he remembered so fondly from his childhood: the calming song of rain hitting glass.

The sound clip lasted only a few seconds, but Frank was already sold. Back on the main page, where he once again studied the list, he read the text accompanying the hyperlink (some of them had these short blurbs; others didn't). It was brief, and seemingly vague, but something about the words made Frank feel better about purchasing something from such a tacky little website:

listen to the rain sing from another place

It was wistful, even oddly poetic, and Frank wasted no time in entering his credit card details to buy the sound file. Within minutes, it was happily downloading onto his hard drive, and Frank was rummaging in a drawer for his old MP3 player – a gift from Kayla last Christmas.

The Ghost of Rain

Once he was finished, Frank went back downstairs and sat next to his wife. She was watching a soap opera, some American thing about a family of bankers living in a big house filled with secrets.

Frank shuffled closer to Kayla. She smiled vacantly, and moved along the sofa an inch. Away from him. "I found one," he said, staring at the side of her face, at the skin of her cheek where the television light was reflected like a multicoloured rash.

"Hmmm? What's that, love?" She kept watching the screen, her eyes glassy.

"I found a recording of rain. It's on my player, now, ready for this evening."

"That's good," she said, nodding her head and pursing her lips. "I'm glad."

Frank stood and walked through into the kitchen, where he opened the fridge and took out the bottle of wine Kayla had opened half an hour ago. It was almost empty; she had been hitting it hard. He recalled his father's tired face; the way the old man had downed a bottle of vodka every night before raging at the walls, at Frank's mother, and even at Frank himself. Slowly, he reached into the cabinet above the work bench and took out a glass, poured himself a drink, and returned the bottle to its place on the shelf. Kayla would open another bottle when this one was empty; he knew she would. She usually did.

He stood in the doorway, waiting for her to acknowledge him. Kayla stared at the screen, at the capering idiots who were badly acting out fictional lives. He waited a while longer, wishing that he could think of something to say. Then, finally, he gave up and turned away, heading towards the other door that led to the stairs. "I'm going in the bath," he said, knowing that she wouldn't answer.

He lay in the tub for a long time, reading the poetry book and wondering what had gone wrong lately. Kayla was struggling to find work. Her position had gone from being an in-demand freelance illustrator to begging for scraps and doing assignments for free, just to keep on the radar. His own job was beginning to seem less stable with each week that passed, and every time he read the word "recession" in the papers he closed his eyes and tried to blot it out.

The bath water was cooling down, but still it was comfortable enough to lie in. Frank placed his book on the shelf at the side of the bath and looked at his hands. The skin was drawing in, tightening, becoming prune-like, but he didn't yet feel the urge to leave the water. Perhaps if he stayed there all night, Kayla might snap out of it and realise that he was missing.

A dog barked somewhere outside; someone yelled a name; a car horn blared for what seemed like minutes, and then abruptly stopped, as if sick of the sound of its own alarm.

Frank felt the obscure yet powerful urge to weep. It came from deep within him, a reservoir contained beneath his skin and his bones, and it took all of his strength to deny the tears the entry they demanded. Instead, he let his body slip beneath the surface of the lukewarm water, covering his face and his nose, obscuring his view of the room. He stayed there for as long as he could, straining for breath and listening to the dull, hollow sound of his own heartbeat, and when he was forced to resurface it felt like he had let something important slip out of his grasp.

ii. the listening

Kayla was already in bed by the time he turned in. It was late – after 1 AM – and he felt shredded, as if his body had been lacerated by tiny blades. The bath hadn't helped; he didn't feel clean. Tiredness mocked him; it smothered him, making him stumble as he entered the bedroom, and then whisked away, leaving him wide-eyed and confused by its sudden absence.

He held the MP3 player in his hand; the headphones were wrapped around his fingers. He crossed the room in darkness, not wanting to disturb Kayla by turning on the light. Why should both of them suffer because of his inability to sleep?

He didn't bother to put on his sleeping shorts, just climbed into bed naked. Kayla's body moved involuntarily away from his touch, and she turned over onto her side, as if trying to escape his proximity. Frank looked at her back, at the freckles across her shoulders and the small tattoo at the nape of her neck. It was a tiny butterfly, something she'd had done years before they had even met.

Trying not to shift the mattress or the pillows too much, he slid under the covers. Lying there, stiff as a corpse, he fumbled with the player, carefully untwining the headphone wire and trying to locate the button that would switch on the machine. He put the plastic buds in his ears and continued to pass his thumb across the unit, until at last he felt the countersunk button. He pressed it and waited, not expecting much from this but at the same time desperate for it to help.

The Ghost of Rain

At first he heard very little, just a soft hiss, like telephone static. Then, gradually, it was displaced and replaced by a more insistent and irregular noise. This, he realised, was the start of the rain. He recognised it at once; it was the sound of memory, of safety and sanctuary. Long ago, during his darkest hours, the sound had represented a retreat from the world of anger and drunkenness into which he had been born.

He listened to it for a while, eyes closed and enjoying the feel of it in his ears. It was an odd sensation – a physical one – and it took several moments for him to get used to the vibrations in the shells of his ears. Then, once he had accepted it, and poised on the verge of sleep, the sound became reality and it flooded him, filling him up with its song.

At that point, Frank fell into the deepest sleep he had experienced in months.

He dreamed, of course, of rainfall. He was in a glass room, and could see darkness all around. Everywhere, as far as the eye could see, was the slashing rainy blackness of a night without end – a night that belonged to the past. He watched the rain as it struck the windows, making patterns that he recognised from his childhood. The sound it made as it kissed the glass was nothing short of miraculous: a personal miracle, one that proved to him the existence of a presence that just might be divine. Something was moving out there, in the rain, but he couldn't quite make out what it was or how many there were. He was safe here, in the glass room. Nothing could touch him.

But when he woke, it was to confusion. He struggled up from sleep, unused to its clingy grasp, and fought to get back to his bed, his room, his wife. Gasping for breath, he felt an acute pain in his left ear, and his hand came up to flap at the area. When he realised where he was – and that he was safe – he opened his eyes and stared at the ceiling. A scream was frozen on his lips, stillborn, and he clamped them shut to ensure that it didn't slip out. The headphone wire had become tangled in the night, wrapping around his neck, and one of the buds had slipped from its position. The other one – the left one – had been pushed deep inside his ear, where it grated against the cartilage. Smiling despite his discomfort, Frank plucked the bud from his ear and sat up, resting his back against the headboard. Kayla was still asleep at his side, turned away from him. Rogue sunlight bled through the blinds and touched her hair; golden fingers clutching at her tatty tresses.

Frank put the player on the bedside cabinet, beside the book of poetry and an empty water glass. He stared at it, amazed that he had actually slept. It had worked; he had gone under, lulled by the re-corded sound of rainfall.

"Honey." He reached out and touched Kayla's bare shoulder. She twitched, again moving away from him, putting an extra inch between them. "I slept, love. I've been to sleep."

Kayla turned to face him, her features flattened from sleep, and blinked. She looked different somehow – as if she had been replaced in the night. Then, her face regaining its natural shape, she smiled. Her eyelids flickered. "Did you? Really? That's good."

"It worked. Your idea *worked*." He felt silly for being so enthusiastic, but the rest had given him a burst of energy that he could barely handle. "You're a genius!"

She blinked again, uncertain. "Idea? My idea?"

"The recording. The rain. It worked."

"Ah, yes. I remember." She lay on her back, eyes closing. "I remember." Then she was once again lost in the folds of sleep.

Frank got out of bed, showered, and dressed in a clean suit. This morning felt special; it felt different. Everything had taken on an extra dimension, as if he were truly seeing things for the first time. Household objects – the wardrobe, the television on the corner shelf, the books scattered around the bed – no longer looked so prosaic. They looked...*glorious*.

He left the house early, planning to arrive at the office before anyone else and get things done – outstanding filing, responding to emails, drafting letters prior to them being sent off to the typist. Traffic was light, and even when he briefly joined the motorway (a point where usually he was caught up in queues) his journey was unimpeded. He reached out and turned on the radio, tuning it to a local station, but the speakers emitted only a low, hushed static.

Frowning, he glanced at the digital readout. There were no numbers visible, just red streaks across the tiny rectangular screen.

The static sounded like distant rainfall.

He turned off the radio and drove the rest of the way in silence, subtly disturbed by what he had heard. More than an echo of last night's recording, it had sounded like a continuation of the same rain, as if it had followed him from sleeping to waking.

Frank shook off the thought and steered the car through the Leeds one-way system, snatching his parking ticket from the automatic machine at the top of the ramp, and heading into the underground car park. There were a lot of empty spaces – more than normal. He knew that some of these were empty simply because he was early, but some of them had previously held cars belonging to staff made redundant in the recent cull.

He pulled into his space and turned off the engine, throwing back his head and sinking into the seat. He stared at the concrete walls, straining to hear the traffic noise beyond, but succeeded only in catching the distant sound of fluid splashing against something solid. His left ear ached; the pain had subsided but not vanished. There was a gentle ache, and if he focused on it he began to hear a phantom of the recording which had guided him to sleep.

Climbing out of the car, he headed towards the exit. He rode the lift in silence, trying not to hear the gentle hissing of the cables above the car.

Once in the main office, he took off his jacket and strode towards his cubicle. He glimpsed a couple of other heads bowed down to desks, but no-one looked up to greet him. Since the job losses, it was as if any sense of camaraderie between workers had been severed. It was every man for himself and each morning when Frank walked in there it felt like someone had passed away and no funeral announcement was forthcoming.

His initial good mood now shattered, Frank spent the morning pretending to work. For some reason his moods were up and down; it felt like some kind of depression, but why would it suddenly occur to him today, when he had finally managed to get some rest? Nothing made sense – but that was the way of things now. The world had proved to be a different place to the one in which he had begun to believe, and tendrils of his childhood seemed to be creeping out of the past to caress him.

"Lunch?"

Frank looked up from his desk, where he had been trying to read a report that made less sense as the day dragged on. "Huh?"

Maria smiled down at him, but her expression was filled with a sadness that he had been unable to fathom in the three years he had known her. "It's lunchtime. Fancy a trip to the café?"

Frank nodded, stood, and walked behind her towards the lift. Her shoes whispered on the carpet tiles, and he didn't want to think about what the sound reminded him of.

"You're in an odd funk today." Maria stood in front of the lift doors, waiting for them to open. "Were you in early, too? That's not like you."

He smiled. "Yeah. Don't know what came over me."

Maria shuffled closer to him, and not for the first time the thought crossed his mind that she felt more for him than simple friendship. There was something in the way she looked at him, or stood near him, that always made him suspect that she was attracted to him; but he hadn't felt worthy of such attention for a long time.

"You're quiet. What's up?" She cocked her head like an expectant puppy.

"Oh, just the usual. Kayla's being a bit funny; I'm worried about what's happening here at work. You know. The usual shit."

The Ghost of Rain

The lift doors opened and for a moment Frank expected rain to be falling in there, such was the sound that threatened to fill his ears. He was filled with a calm expectancy, like the feeling before a storm, when you expect a downpour. The lift, of course, was dry; the shiny interior was no different than usual.

"Come on," said Maria. "Sandwiches are on me today."

During the downward journey, Frank glanced at Maria. She was a good-looking woman, he knew that. Lots of men around the building gave her lustful gazes, and one or two of them had even asked her out. Maria had not once accepted a date; she always turned them down, politely but firmly. Frank knew that she was single – in fact she had not been in a long-term relationship in all the time they'd known each other, just brief flings and a memorable one-night stand that had almost ended in violence.

Again, he wondered if she felt something for him; then, ashamed, he reminded himself that he was nothing to write home about, and that a woman had not come on to him in over a decade. Ego; that's all it was. A silly workplace fantasy.

In that moment he felt a crushing loneliness that welled up from somewhere he could not even begin to imagine. Like liquid, it filled his arms and legs, his torso; and then, finally, it filled his skull. When the lift doors opened he staggered out into the lobby, thankfully a few paces behind Maria so she didn't witness his struggle. He shook his head and mentally righted himself, then followed her out into the street.

The Ghost of Rain

Again, his mind and body expected it to be raining. Despite the fact that he had seen no rain smeared on the huge lobby windows, everything about him had automatically been ready to step into a downpour. The world, to him, felt poised constantly on the verge of rainfall, and it was disorienting to be reminded all the time that the rain was not in evidence. His hands prepared for moisture that didn't come; his hair flattened under the pressure of an invisible storm.

Inside the café, they sat down to coffee and sandwiches. Frank stared out of the window, poised for the rain, and Maria watched him.

"Come on," she said. "Tell me what's really wrong." There was rain behind her voice; a gentle liquid swirl.

He put down his coffee, turned from the window, and looked into her eyes. Her rainy, rainy eyes. "Last night I went to sleep listening to this recording – it was rain, just the rain. I downloaded it from some dodgy website."

Maria sipped her coffee. Her long fingers flexed around the cup. "What, like a tape recording or something? Of rain?" She smiled; then, when she realised that he was serious, the smile faltered, fell.

"On my MP3 player. It's a sound file. You know – like those music files you can buy now instead of CDs." There was a sense of time slipping away; of history unwinding from a central mass, like orange peel.

"Okay, so you listened to this recording of rain…and?"

"And now I'm being haunted." He didn't know where the words had come from, only that they were true. He had not even considered this a haunting before he had spoken, but now it all made sense. "I'm being haunted by the ghost of rain."

Maria looked shaken. Her eyes flicked around the room; her hand trembled as she put down her cup. "I don't know what you mean. What are you talking about?"

Frank closed his eyes. "It's like every time I step outside I'm expecting it to be raining, and when it isn't I feel sad, depressed. My whole body – my soul – is expecting to feel rain against my skin, my cheeks, and when it doesn't a part of me dies. I need the rain. I need to hear it, to feel it, to taste it." Spoken aloud, it seemed absurd, yet he knew that it was the truth, the hidden truth of his situation. "I hear rainfall. Not all the time, but snatches of it, like music on a radio someone just turned on. And it's getting clearer, getting closer. Part of me can't wait until it's here, but the rest of me…the rest of me is fucking terrified of what will happen when it arrives."

Maria said nothing for a while. She sipped her coffee. She played with the crusts on her sandwich. Then, finally, she took a deep breath. "Listen, Frank, I know things have been shit at work, and we're all worried about losing our jobs…and I know that you and Kayla haven't been getting on for a while."

"I'm not having a breakdown, if that's what you think." He glared at her, but couldn't hold it for longer than a moment.

"I know. Just hear me out. You're under a lot of strain – shit, everyone is these days. All I'm saying is. Well, what I'm trying to say is that…I'm here. If you need me. You don't have to go through all this on your own." She reached out and grasped his hand, squeezing his fingers.

"I..." Frank looked at her hand resting on his, staring at her small, pale fingers, her narrow wrist. Then he looked up, into her rain-filled eyes, and tried to smile. The sound of distant rainfall came to him from across the café, and when he concentrated on the sound he thought that it was drawing near.

Soon, he thought, *the rain will fall.*

iii. the drowned ones

That night Frank listened to the recording again. All afternoon, after his discussion with Maria, he had been looking forward to hearing it again. It was like a drug, and he craved it. It was that simple; that prosaic. He knew that when he heard the recording, everything would become clear, and that his mind would be opened to new possibilities.

Kayla was asleep. He lay down next to her, leaving a gap between them, and slipped the hard little ear buds into place. He paused for a moment before switching it on, the anticipation almost unbearable. Then, when the sound of the rain filled his ears, he closed his eyes and allowed himself to drift away.

This time the rain was closer. Before, the first time, it had sounded far away, as if he were separated from it by several rooms. Now it sounded like it was right outside, beyond the glass upon which it lashed and splattered. He imagined that he was back in his childhood bedroom, the sound of the rain drowning out the yells and shrieks of his parents. He couldn't hear the plates and glasses being thrown; the sound of a fist hitting bone was beyond him.

The Ghost of Rain

The rain surged. It was not a steady sound; it seemed to rush towards him, and then, at the last minute, it would retreat, as if afraid of making contact. This rain, it was a living thing; an entity with its own drives and desires. There was intelligence at work here, and to hear it was to draw closer to something numinous...something strong and bold and terrifying.

Yes, it *was* terrifying, like an animal in the wild: a lion or a tiger, ready to pounce and kill at any moment. There was something unfathomable about the rain, and it was this quality which made it beautiful. Sleep reached out to him, striving across the washed-out landscape of his psyche. He waited for it to arrive, and as he lay there on the bed, his eyes squeezed tightly shut, he felt the ghost of rain on his cheeks. He didn't panic; he just let it come, becoming more real as he drifted into slumber.

This time it was not a dream. It was reality; he was there, in the other place. He didn't know where it was, but it was raining there, always raining. Darkness billowed beyond the opaque sheets of rain, and shapes moved within it. He did not strain to see them; in time, he would be allowed a glimpse of whatever stalked there, waiting for him to join them. He knew that as much as he knew the rain was real.

Then, like fragments of a rogue transmission, he heard voices beneath the rain. They were low, murmuring, but it sounded like a form of prayer. Several voices chanted the same thing, but it was too quiet for him to make out any words, and he suspected that it wasn't even English anyway. So he let the sounds flow over and around him: the gentle thrum of the rain, and the voices wrapped like threads within it. The light was the colour of old grey sacks. The ground beneath his feet was sodden.

Then, much too soon, it was morning, and Frank was rising towards yet another day. He tried to hang on to that other place, grabbing strands of sleep, but his rain-slicked hands lost their grip and he faltered, coming awake in sunlight. The disappointment he felt was huge, like a dark cloud hanging over him, but he took comfort in the fact that he could return there, as long as he possessed the recording.

"I brought you some coffee." Kayla walked into the room, still dressed in her night clothes. Her legs looked thin, like two sticks hanging below the hem, and her skin was the colour of old bones. He had never seen her look so frail, and for a moment wondered if he were to blame.

"What's wrong with us?" he looked at her, but didn't take the cup.

"We're broken," she said, looking down at the floor. "We're busted and I don't know how to fix us."

"When did it happen? Why did it happen?" He sat there on the bed, helpless and alone, knowing exactly what she was about to say. It was not some amazing insight; deep down, he had known the truth all along.

"I've been seeing someone. He makes me...well, not happy. Not that. He makes me less sad." Still she could not meet his gaze.

Frank reached out and took the cup. His hand was steady. He wished that he could hear the rain, if only for a few seconds, to clear his thoughts. "Do you want to leave me?"

"Yes. No. I'm not sure." Her hands were restless, the fingers forming knots at her waist. She shifted her balance from one foot to the other, and then, when she realised what she was doing, she made an effort to remain still. "What do you want?" At last, she looked up and into his eyes. Frank heard the distant splash of rainfall.

He looked at the cup, then at her face. "I don't even know what I want, not anymore. Everything's so weird now, like I'm living through someone else's dreams." He took a sip of coffee; it was cold.

Kayla left the house as soon as she was dressed, not telling him where she was going. He guessed that she was meeting the man she had been sleeping with – he had heard her on the phone earlier, whispering and crying. He hoped that she could find whatever it was that she needed.

He put in his headphones and listened to the rain. It didn't sound any closer, nor did it seem any farther away. It was there, right there, on the other side of the glass. If he closed his eyes, he could make out huge floor-to-ceiling windows, and the rain hammering against the panes. It was *his* place, a refuge: the place he had always kept locked deep inside, but which was now struggling towards the surface, to merge with the world around him. He wondered what would happen when both these worlds met – the inner and the outer – and was afraid that there might be some kind of adverse reaction, like when two toxic chemicals were poured into the same dish.

Perhaps, he thought, *it will all end when the edges meet, when the barriers come down and the rain seeps in through the cracks.*

He recalled those figures in the rain, and the way that they had moved around him. He had not registered it last night, but they had formed a circle around him, and their chants had carved out a rhythm from the rain, becoming part of its song. The figures had stood on two legs, but he had known immediately that they were not human. They were the inhabitants of that other place – the place where it rained forever, and where the hollows in the rain formed burrows in which one could hide.

What he didn't know was if the figures wished him well or if they meant him harm. Was their chanting part of some protective ritual, to keep him safe from the storm, or was it some form of attack on his mental armour, an attempt to break him down and create a breach so that the rain could pour on in?

For the first time he began to admit that there was something familiar about the dream: a sense that he had experienced something like it before, perhaps in childhood, during the dark times when he had been forced to hide out in his room like a prisoner. Something clicked, then, a tiny cog falling into place within the larger machinery of his mind.

The rain, the safety he found there. Blood, screams, a red handprint on glass.

He walked the rooms of the house, listening to the rain, trying to piece things together. When nothing came, he sat down and closed his eyes, hoping that the rain would drown him.

Sleep took him without warning, and this time he found himself out in the rain. His hair was plastered to his head and his clothes were soaked through to the skin. The figures paced in a circle around him, their chanting louder this time yet still too quiet to be properly heard.

The Ghost of Rain

The last time he had decided that they moved on two legs, but he had not at that point even considered their other limbs. Bloated torsos sat awkwardly upon skinny lower sections, with a cluster of arms sprouting from each central wad. Like mutated spiders or crustaceans, they lurched through the dark rain, those terrible upper limbs flapping in the air. There were no hands at the ends of the appendages; just hardened spurs or pincers which snapped at the rain, trying to grab the drops as they fell.

Frank wanted to scream, but the dream – or the place – would not allow it. His breath lodged in his throat and his lips refused to open wide enough to let out the sound. The figures pranced on, tottering on those scrawny legs, pincers snip-snapping at empty air, ragged little heads lolling on long, thin stalks of neck...

He woke to the sound of hammering. The headphones had come out of his ears as he slept, and the sound he could make out was that of someone banging on the front door. Could it be Kayla? Had she left behind her key in the rush to leave, and now she wanted to come back and talk?

He ran to the door, tugged it open, and saw Maria standing on the doorstep.

It was dark; he had slept through the day.

"Your hair's wet. Were you in the bath?"

Confused, he raised a hand and ran it through his hair. His palm came away cold and damp to the touch. "Come in," he whispered, stepping back from the door.

He led her through into the living room, and then motioned for her to sit down. She took a seat on the sofa, where he had been sleeping only moments before, and slipped off her coat. "I could use a drink." She smiled, but it was strained.

"I have whisky."

"That's fine." She nodded, pushing her coat onto the back of the sofa.

Frank returned with the drinks, unable to focus on the moment. It seemed like only minutes ago when Kayla had left the house that morning, but now it was dark and Maria was sitting on the sofa, a drink clenched in her tiny fist.

"I'm worried about you," she said. "I came to see if you're okay. I saw Kayla earlier, down the high street. She was...she was with someone, in a car. Kissing him, and crying. I didn't know what to do, or to say." She gulped the whisky, coughing slightly as it went down the wrong way.

"He's her lover. I think she's leaving me." He was pleased to find that it didn't hurt as much as it once would have. The pain was distant and fleeting, like something that had happened a long time ago.

The sound of the rain suddenly filled his ears. It had never really left. Frank knew that he no longer needed the recording; the rain was inside him, and it always had been. When he was a boy, hiding in his room, he had absorbed it into his body, drinking it down through his pores.

"You can tell me anything," said Maria, crossing her legs. "You know that, don't you?"

The rain surged, breaking through, and outside it began to fall from the sky. He glanced at the windows, at the rain sloshing down the glass, and knew that Maria was right, he could tell her everything: he could tell it all, at last.

"Wow, it's really coming down out there." She turned to the window, her face highlighted by the reflected downfall, and then back to Frank. Her eyes were filled with water.

"You can see it? You can see the rain?"

She nodded. "I think I always could. Ever since I've known you, there's been a storm brewing, and now it's finally here."

He closed his eyes, and then opened them again, wanting to see exactly what happened to the world when the rain broke through.

"When I was a boy, just ten years old, I killed my father." Something dripped onto his scalp. He looked up, at the ceiling, and saw water squeezing through a crack in the plaster. "He used to beat up my mother, and sometimes he'd hit me. One night things went too far, and I killed him. I pushed him down the stairs, and he went through the glass doors...out into the rain."

Blood, screams, a red handprint on glass. A garbled curse issued from a mouth filled with rain – not his father's voice, but his mother's, damning the son who had acted in her defence.

"Ever since then it's been raining somewhere, but I could never get close enough to hear. Then, when I found the recording, it gave me a way back into that other place – the place where all our bad deeds are stored, and where we make penance for what we've done, or what we think we've done."

More cracks opened in the walls and ceiling; the windows began to shatter, but slowly, deliberately. Rain started to fall inside the house, soaking everything. It fell on Frank, and on Maria, but neither of them noticed it. They only had eyes for each other. The room turned monochrome, like a scene from a black and white film. Or like his grey, grey childhood.

"It wasn't your fault. You were just a kid..." She was weeping now, but her tears just blended with the rain.

"It's always *someone's* fault."

Figures entered the room, forming a circle around him. He wasn't sure if Maria could even see them, but they were there, the dwellers in the rainfall, the drowned ones: the awful rainy day creatures that must be faced, must *always* be faced in the end. Their graceless ungulae snapped towards him; their bulbous bodies twitched and shivered through the wavering screen of rain. Then, abruptly, they fell silent and simply waited for him to say his goodbyes. There was no mercy here, no safety from the storm. Every storm, he knew at last, must be confronted, and at the end of each life some rain must fall...

"I have to go now. They've come for me." He began to move towards the nearest figure, wincing at the sight of it as it came into view. Its face was pale and mottled, like burlap sacking thrown into a river, and the waterlogged skin had sagged and creased around the base of its thin, quivering neck. The eyes were milky white; the lips were white strands of exposed muscle. It turned towards him, and he couldn't be sure if it was smiling or screaming...

Behind the wall of rain, and beyond the painful memories of a tainted childhood, these things had always been waiting for him – waiting in the rain, or in the streaks and funnels formed by the unending downpour he had set into motion so many years ago.

This was not payback or vengeance; it was simply the way of things, the conclusion to events set in motion during another, similar storm. It was not fair, it was not just, but it was happening. It was here.

"No...come back." Maria's voice was muffled, as if underwater. "It wasn't your fault!"

But he didn't turn back; he carried on, into the deluge, glad that he could finally face what had happened. There was no question of blame, just a hunger which must be sated and gaping mouths to be fed. The forces summoned here did not recognise human justifications. All they wanted was to claim what they now owned – his life, his soul, even his memories.

The mumbling figures moved forward to close the circle, resuming their chants and grabbing him with those razor-sharp pincers. The last thing Frank felt before he was torn apart was the wet smack of rain on his face.

Gary McMahon's fiction has appeared in magazines and anthologies in the U.K. and U.S and has been reprinted in both THE MAMMOTH BOOK OF BEST NEW HORROR and THE YEAR'S BEST FANTASY & HORROR. He is the British-Fantasy-Award-nominated author of Rough Cut, All Your Gods Are Dead, Dirty Prayers, How to Make Monsters, Rain Dogs, Different Skins, Pieces of Midnight, The Harm, Hungry Hearts, and has edited an anthology of original novelettes titled We Fade to Grey.

Forthcoming and current publications include several reprints in "Best of" anthologies, a story in the mass market anthology THE END OF THE LINE, the novels Pretty Little Dead Things and Dead Bad Things from Angry Robot/Osprey and The Concrete Grove trilogy from Solaris.

Website: www.garymcmahon.com

Berlin Sushi

Benedict. J. Jones

The guns boom and crack in the distance, the sky is lit up like flashes in a pan and I sit in the dark waiting for Ivan. My mother put me into the attic and told me to stay there. I'm only fifteen but I know what the Russians will do to me if they find me: what they'll try and do to all the women of Berlin. Frantic shouting echoes up from the street and I peek through the small window. Men in camouflage smocks, feld grau blouses and over-coats move into the street and begin hiding. Their officer barks orders at them like a head chef making sure his kitchen is in order before service and within moments they have vanished as though they were the meat from the soup my mother has made for the last year.

I see my first Ivan an hour later. The newsreels were right he looks like one of Ghengis Khan's Mongols descending on us from the steppes. The gun in his hands had an ammunition clip shaped like a banana, not that I'd know a banana if I saw one any more, and a thick fur cap sat upon his head. He looked up and down the street before motion-ing back from whence he had came. An engine roared and a tank jerked around the corner. A dozen Ivans were clinging to the shell of the metal beast and another half dozen of their comrades moved warily along the pavement. The tank was half way down the street when a machine gun began chattering. Two of the smocked men emerged from a cellar and fired their Panzerfausts at the side of the tank. There was a great bang and a crack like wet celery being snapped in half. The tank jerked forward once and stopped. I put my hands over my ears as the machine gun continued to chatter. The Russians fired back and began to run back down the street. The great gun on the tank boomed once and the Millers house at the end of the street shook as the front wall collapsed. The machine gun fell silent. The crew of the tank bailed out and ran after their comrades.

The Russians came back twenty minutes later pushing a big green field gun. They blasted the houses where the German soldiers had hidden themselves and dropped grenades into the cellars. When they were done they searched some of the houses and came out holding curtains, dresses and watches; their faces like those of child raiders who had forced the lock on a sweetshop. Then they broke down the door to my house.

I watched through a gap in the floorboards as the laughing Ivans threw my mother around the kitchen and made her dance with them. They emptied the cutlery into their bedrolls and one even took our good soup bowl. At the end of the dance she lay on the floor - her legs white and spread as though she were a chicken waiting to be stuffed. They took turns stuffing her. There were fifteen of them. I counted. When they were finished and leaving one remained. He walked back to my mother and struck her in the head with the butt of his machine gun. Then he climbed back on her and stuffed her one last time. When he was done she had gone the colour of icing and didn't move anymore. The Ivan kicked her and left.

.

After an hour I climbed down and rearranged her skirts so that she was covered. I took her recipe book from the bottom drawer and snuck out into the street. There was nothing more I could do for her. The cold pale thing, like a piece of leftover pork, that lay in the kitchen was no longer my mummy.

I moved slowly down the street expecting an Ivan with his britches down behind every wall and corner. There were none. The gunfire popping a few streets away made me think of the fat cracking and spitting as a joint roasted. My stomach spoke to me in low grunts and grumbles as I picked my way across the rubble which now covered the pavements. I looked up and stopped. A great, tawny, lion padded across the top of the intersection in front of me. He regarded me strangely before padding on to sniff at the charred corpse of a Volksturm volunteer who lay on the broken bricks and masonry. I closed my eyes and felt like that made me invisible to this roving king. But I couldn't keep my eyes shut and peeked from beneath my lids. The great beast looked from the corpse to me and back again for a minute before it moved on. I watched the swish of its tail until it vanished behind the burnt out shell of a truck. I closed my eyes once more and felt my cloak of invincible invisibility fall once more over me and I dropped to my knees in front of the roasted corpse. I stayed there for a long time.

Berlin Sushi

The Russians had already been at Kristina's house, her dress was torn and one of her eyes bruised, but her and her mother welcomed me in. We sat in the dark as the gunfire began to recede. Shouting in the street dragged us awake but the shouts were quickly silenced by a single gunshot. Hunger stabbed at my stomach like toothpicks in a club sandwich and the soles of my shoes began to look as tasty as freshly sliced beef.

We learned to go out early in the morning and scavenge for water and food while the Ivans slept off their hangovers. At night we sat quiet in the dark as packs of them swaggered around the streets drinking and firing their guns in the air. Once one of them tried the door but we had pushed a bureau against it and he soon cursed at us in bad German before stomping off in search of easier sport.

Kristina and I barely spoke until the Tommys arrived. She would just sit in the corner with dark rings growing beneath her eyes. The Tommys eyes weren't as hard as those of the Ivans and sometimes they would give us chocolate and try to help us. I kept my distance but the chocolate was nice. Kristina's house was on the edge of the new British zone so we still saw the Ivans, especially at night, roving in their packs on a hunt for women and loot. In their own way the Tommys were as bad as the Ivans but at least they were nicer about it; victorious soldiers always want the same things.

Within a couple of weeks Kristina had three boyfriends; two

Tommys and an Ivan. Even the Ivan was nice, his name was Alex, and they all brought food for us. The canned meat tasted like ashes in my mouth and I found it hard to keep the potatoes down. Kristina told me that one of her Tommys – Jack - had a friend, George, who wanted to meet me. My ears turned the colour of beetroot at the thought. She had told him I was nineteen. George brought me flowers. Kristina lent me her blue dress and George took me to a bar filled with other Tommys. It was nice but when he went to kiss me I ran back into the house. George wasn't angry he just laughed and said he'd see me the next day. Kristina didn't come home that night.

They found her the next day in the ruins of an old bank. She had been lain out on the concrete like a carcass on a butchers slab. The Hitler Jurgen dagger that had done the work was still in her side. She still had the remnants of her yellow dress but her shoes and nylons were gone. A neighbour told me that they didn't find all of her.

George took me out again two days later and this time as we walked home from the bar he pushed against me in a door way. Fumes hung on his breath and his groin swelled as he pressed his body against mine. I smiled and he told me how beautiful I was. He leant in close, lips as red as the essence that drips from rare steak, and I stretched up towards him. My teeth sank into his cheek as the army bayonet I had had concealed in my hand bag slid into his stomach as easily as if it were butter. George sank to his knees and fell forward.

I spat out the remnants of his cheek.

I prefer the more tender cuts from the rump and thighs. As I cut into him I remember back to that charred corpse in the street that first sweet taste of cooked flesh. I begin to feel full for the first time since Kristina and it is a wonderful feeling. I gorge myself. The world is a different place now and a girl with a beautiful smile can go anywhere. George was nice to me and he tastes like chicken I'll always remember him.

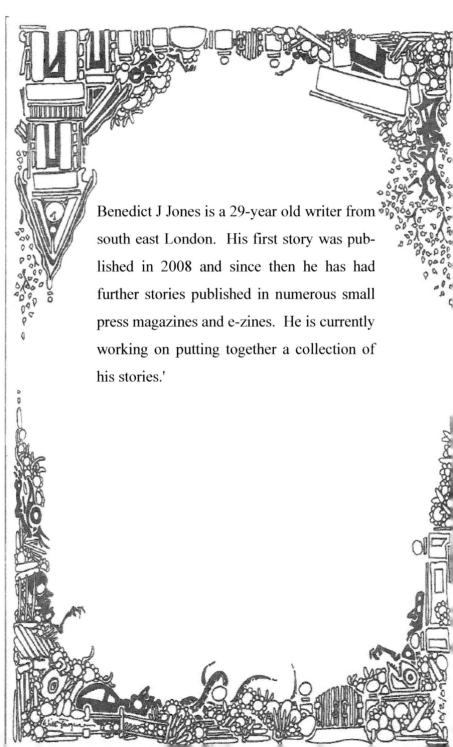

Benedict J Jones is a 29-year old writer from south east London. His first story was published in 2008 and since then he has had further stories published in numerous small press magazines and e-zines. He is currently working on putting together a collection of his stories.'

The House of Constant Shadow

Stephen Bacon

The newspaper made much of how the dog was killed, taking great delight in describing the level of blood that must have pooled in the garden, explaining where the various bits of the animal were found. As Ernest read the story to his wife he cradled her in his arms and comforted her distraught tears, shed for the loss of her beloved pet. Margaret had taken the stray in five years ago, and she'd cherished him like the grand-child they'd never had. The newspaper was lurid in its description of what had happened; deliberating as to what kind of psychopath could commit such an atrocity. It speculated about the desperate fight the dog must have put up, warning readers to be on the lookout for someone with considerably bloodstained clothing. As Ernest tried to quell his wife's sobs, he thought about how long it had taken him to rinse his coat and trousers that morning as she slept, recalling the popping sound as the knife entered the fur - and remembered Tramp's bulging eyes as he'd stood over him and watched the final breaths shiver away.

Of course, Margaret assumed the dog had been killed by the Farnhams from next door. She said as much to the policeman who attended on the morning of the massacre. Ernest was hesitant about going into too much detail, but the officer seemed interested to hear about the year-long feud, enthusiastically writing in his notepad.

After he'd gone, Ernest made a nice cup of sweet tea and questioned the wisdom of mentioning the grudge between the Farnhams and them. Margaret shook in rage, and yelled, white spittle disturbing the steady movement of dust motes in the morning sunshine. He returned his manner to that of the supportive husband and hurried back to the kitchen, while Margaret jerked the curtains closed again.

They lived in a neat terraced house in the centre of Sheffield, loomed over by a grotesque football stadium, perpetually in shadows. In 1965 when they'd moved in, the ground was little more than a pleasant walled lawn with a couple of terraces at either end. A rise up the leagues had swollen the attendances, bloating the size of the stadium to massive proportions, like a wart upon an otherwise unblemished patch of skin.

The House of Constant Shadow

Ernest spent as much time as possible in the sanctuary of his garden, an escape from the labours of husbandry. The well-tended flowers and shrubs were, he felt, a reflection of the owner within. And it was a great place to catch a glimpse of Eleanor.

Eleanor was their neighbour; single, mid to late twenties, short dark hair. He sometimes saw her returning home from the gym, all flushed and glowing in tight-fitting clothes. He'd pruned many roses to the sound of Eleanor showering, the bewitching noise reaching him through the open window of her bathroom.

But the real problem was the family that lived on the other side – the Farnhams. Layabout father, fishwife mother, two thuggish, constantly-hooded sons, and a daughter who dressed like she was 18 but had only just started secondary school. Probably wouldn't be long before she ended up pregnant. Margaret decided very early on that she didn't like them, and – as was always the case –whatever Margaret *didn't* like, Ernest *couldn't* like.

It was the week after Tramp's butchering. Margaret usually spent the afternoon wedged into her favourite armchair, munching enormous packets of Doritos as she listened to the radio. She called occasionally to Ernest, rousing him from the garden to attend to her needs – the odd drink, another packet of crisps, sometimes just to turn the volume up.

It is a myth that the blind have excellent hearing. At least, it was in Margaret's case. She had been totally without sight since 1964, yet she still needed the radio on at full volume. Ernest didn't mind – it masked his own pursuit of self enjoyment. From downstairs came the sound of Neil Diamond, as Ernest crouched in the back bedroom. He poked the lens of his camera against the window and fired off a few discreet shots of Eleanor hanging out her washing in the back garden. The way she stood on tiptoe to peg an item of clothing made Ernest tremble slightly.

The house was permanently dark so Ernest drew the curtains after he'd finished, and packed away his camera. He stumbled over something at the top of the stairs and swore under his breath. The uncomfortable volume of Dolly Parton rose to meet him as he descended the stairs. He stood for a moment in the doorway, watching Margaret's huge chins wobble as she snored, almost as if she was competing with *Jolene*. It was time for her tea, and there would be trouble again if it was late. He ghosted into the kitchen.

It was usually the best-lit room in the house because there was nothing outside to obscure the sunlight, and it poured through the glass like a warm companion. Ernest busied himself with cooking bacon and eggs.

Presently Margaret's snoring reached a crescendo and she snorted, coughing herself awake.

"Ernie!"

"I'm here, love." He hurried into the room. She was dabbing a pool of saliva from the corner of her mouth. "What time is it?" Her sunken eyes were restlessly twitching. "Is it tea-time?"

"I'm on with it, love." He carefully turned down the volume of the radio, strategically timing it as one song finished and another started.

"Turn it down, Ernie," she said. "It's too bloody loud!"

Ernest glared at her and switched the volume to a moderate level. "I thought you liked it loud." His voice was placatory and warm. The only thing spoiling the effect was his middle finger raised towards her unseeing eyes.

"What's for tea? I'm starving." Even without the dimness of the room, she wouldn't see Ernest's gesture. She never did. The accident hadn't just blinded her; it had robbed her of every single speckle of light – NLP, the doctors called it.

"Your favourite, Margaret -" He also raised the index finger, creating an obscene V, and waved that in front of her face. "- bacon and eggs."

"Hurry up then." She belched, pulling a sour face.

Ernest could smell the cheesy aroma staining the air so he shuffled back into the kitchen to be embraced by the sizzling bacon. Now the radio was low he could hear cars out on the street, and the voices of children on their way home from school. It was always jarring and disappointing to encounter people with their whole lives ahead of them.

A loud thumping sound reverberated through the wall. It was the Farnhams, probably complaining about the music. Ernest winced.

"I've just fucking turned it down!" Margaret's voice was almost unrecognisable, distorted by rage.

Since the police had questioned the Farnhams about Tramp, the feud had escalated. They had stepped up their campaign of hate.

Ernest rushed the rest of the tea, in an attempt to smooth over Margaret's mood. The bacon was too undercooked for her liking, but she didn't seem to grumble too much.

The House of Constant Shadow

Later on, Margaret turned on the television to listen to some of the soap operas. Ernest mumbled some excuse about re-potting a shrub in the back garden, and escaped outside.

The summer evening was warm and still. Ernest waited about half an hour until he was sure that Margaret was asleep or deeply engrossed in the television, before he slipped out the back gate and used the phone box at the end of the road. It was a quick call, and then he returned to the house, fussing attentively around Margaret. He made her a cup of tea and dissolved three paracetamols into it - all the better to induce sleepiness – and set it on the tray before her, next to a large packet of chocolate biscuits. Then he was back in the garden, breathing the air, watching the sky darkening as dusk descended upon the city, clouds fading from crimson rags to the dull purple hue of bruises.

He was struck by a strange sight; the property opposite, whose back faced his own – a dilapidated terraced that stood hunched between the adjoining houses – had two people in the garden, separated by the width of the rear access track. It had lain empty for many years; the grimy windows were testament to the absence of life. Ernest watched the couple for several minutes. There was something strangely familiar about their movement; some facet of their gait, a vaguely recognisable

47

lilt to their voice. He frowned as he tried to ponder his puzzlement, but the notion soon evaporated, unanswered, into the ether.

In the small wooden shed at the end of his garden, behind the racks of discarded bric-a-brac and junk, a metal tin lay hidden among the dust. Ernest quickly unlocked the tin's padlock and removed several twenty pound notes from the bundle of money that was rolled together with an elastic band. His 'pleasure fund' was the accumulation of years' worth of squirreling; the odd twenty slipped away from his state pension, a tenner here and there. It soon accumulated.

By now Margaret would be snoring again, he reasoned, so he entered the alley beyond the gate and hurried to his rendezvous.

Half an hour later he was hunched over Crystal in her upstairs flat, the thrusting causing droplets of fluid to run loose from his nose. He felt an immense stab of cramp in his right calf, moments before he ejaculated, groaning into her heavily made-up face, mascara-thick eyes closed, smelling of cheap perfume.

Afterwards they sat in the threadbare chairs and watched television. Ernest dressed himself while Crystal escaped to the greasy bathroom and tidied herself up. When she returned, her makeup had been reapplied, illuminating the beauty of her blue eyes. Ernest had fallen in love with them several years before, the instant he'd first glimpsed them.

Crystal charged by the hour. She still charged the same rate to Ernest, many years after first meeting him. It was always the case that the sex was over in the first ten minutes, and the remaining time was spent in quiet companionship or intimate chat.

They talked pleasantly about what had happened over the past few weeks since Ernest's last visit. Crystal steered the conversation round to a subject about which she had been curious for a while. "Has your wife always been blind, or is it getting worse over the years?"

She felt the atmosphere change, became aware of that strange look on his face, as he turned to gaze at her, seemingly lost in the memories of time. Ages passed, and she almost thought he had ignored the question, but then he suddenly spoke.

"1964 was the final year of my life.

"We'd met at a local dinner and dance a couple of years before. We'd been courting quite seriously. At first I was happy – thought that Margaret was the one I'd spend the rest of my life with. As it turned out, I was right.

"I was 20 then, she was 19. She'd a lovely face, full of life and excitement. But a mate of mine...his sister – Elsie – had started to chat to me whenever we met in the town. I told her I was single. We'd gone out together a couple of times when Margaret had been in Halifax, at her sister's. She'd really turned my head. I was plucking up the courage to end it with Margaret when we had the crash.

"July, 1964. We'd been to Skegness for the day on my motor-bike. I'd planned on talking to her the following weekend. I was excited about seeing Elsie, looking forward to spending time with her, and I was thinking of how I could let Margaret down gently, though I'd no feelings left for her by then.

"The roads through Lincolnshire are winding, and we were heading back in the warm evening. I took a corner too fast and tried to compensate the steering, but we skidded and ended up in the ditch. Margaret was thrown into some bushes and we both blacked out."

Ernest's face was blank. He stared into space, bitterness and regret etched into his wrinkles like a tattoo. A single transparent tear rolled into the creases of his cheek. His voice had changed.

"We were in hospital for a week or so. The doctors couldn't do anything about Margaret's sight – her optic nerve had been damaged. I'd broken my leg and torn a ligament in my arm. Margaret's never seen so much as a flicker of light through her eyes since. She was robbed of her sight, and I lost my happiness that day.

"Of course, I couldn't split up with Margaret then. Call it guilt if you like, but I felt I owed it to make things up to her." Ernest stood and began absently drawing on his jacket, dropping money onto the coffee-table. "And now it's gone full circle and I can only enjoy a life lived in secret."

His house was in darkness; grey-blue light flickered against the walls as Ernest quietly locked the door and whispered into the room. Margaret always insisted that the lights stay off in the house – it saved on the electricity bills – but he could discern her huge form, sleeping in the chair. He stood and watched, his face slack with contempt and abhorrence. Some imperceptible sensation roused her and she stirred, swallowing, and sat up.

"Ernie? That you?"

"Yes, love, it's only me." He laid a hand on her arm. "Let's get you to bed."

The following week passed in a fog of unpleasantness. Someone threw red gloss paint over the Farnhams' front window one night; Ernest awoke a couple of days later to see the contents of his dustbin blowing around the garden; a plastic bag, heavy with numerous dog turds, was thrown against the Farnhams' front door, where it left a stain of evidence.

Saturday night arrived, and Ernest was almost too tired to slip out of bed at 2.30am and masturbate furiously in the spare room, while he listened through the walls to Eleanor's frenzied lovemaking. She usually brought someone home from the nightclub about once a month, giggling drunkenly as they exited the taxi, awakening Ernest in more ways than one. His imagination filled in the blanks that the sound of the sex stirred within him.

Afterwards he noticed a light burning in the bedroom window of the house opposite. His heart almost leapt out of his mouth when he spotted the man facing him across the expanse of the gardens. Ernest was in darkness, so he was sure that he couldn't be seen, but nevertheless he felt bizarrely exposed by the intense nature of the man's scrutiny. The hairs on his neck tingled fiercely. He felt compelled to watch, found it impossible to tear his eyes away from the intriguing figure. The man eventually moved away from the window. Was it just Ernest's imagination, or did a beguiling smirk illuminate the man's face?

The House of Constant Shadow

Before he tiptoed, unsettled, back to bed he remembered to leave a crumpled dressing-gown strewn on the floor, in the hope of tripping Margaret up when she awoke to use the bathroom the next morning.

His life had become a series of petty games, trivial in their execution, nothing more than a catalogue of minor victories, a myriad of unspoken scored points. The dullness that plagued his life – in a physical sense as well as a metaphorical one – was faintly illuminated by these occasional sparks of enjoyment that Ernest managed to ignite. He remembered a quotation from his schooldays – *Thoreau, wasn't it?* – regarding men leading lives of quiet desperation, and he wholly subscribed to this observation. Margaret seemed to remain unaware of the games, and this reinforced his skill and added to the pleasure he gained from them.

A couple of days later he was washing the dishes, basking in the sunlight that graced the kitchen, mentally enjoying his furtive life. He scrubbed at his hands with the scouring pad, attempting to rid his skin of the remnants of red gloss paint that lurked there. He could hear the television. Margaret was listening to Jerry Springer. Ernest decided it was time for her food again, humming to himself as he prepared her toast. He layered the slices with thick butter, sliding the knife across the top to melt it in; all the better to increase the strain upon her already-overburdened heart.

As he entered the room she licked her lips. "Hmmm, that smells nice." Her closed eyes rolled hideously, as if they were convulsing in their sockets. Ernest almost recoiled in disgust, and deliberately jerked the tray down onto her lap, causing the hot tea to slop out of the cup onto her hand.

She let out a yell and snatched her hand away. "Ouch, you clumsy idiot!"

"Sorry, love." His tone masked the smile on his face. "It's because it's so dark in here –"

"Look, it saves us a fortune." She took a bite of toast and chewed noisily. "It's not that dark anyway."

He shook his head at the absurdity of the statement. The curtains were drawn, the television was the only flickering light source. He left her to devour the food.

The garden was cool, the morning sun held back by the bulk of the stadium nearby. He picked up a trowel from an assortment of tools, and began to turn over the soil absently. Slowly his anger leaked away.

The House of Constant Shadow

When he'd lost control of that bike all those years ago he'd also lost control of his life. His happy optimism had been replaced by regretful guilt, their marriage evolving into an arrangement of credits and debits. The children they'd hoped to have - *their* existence died that day too. Instead, an internal bitterness began to grow, like a black seed within his body.

Suddenly he heard a door slamming. Glancing up he saw the father from next door, Farnham, strut past the garden fence. Ernest watched with disdain, noting that for someone with such a debilitating affliction – a crippling bad back – the man managed to struggle to the pub and the bookies regularly enough. Just then the door was yanked open.

"Scott! Fetch me some fags, will you? A ten pack."

He nodded without looking back to acknowledge his wife's words. The door slammed shut again.

Ernest glanced up the street. Soon it would be filled by noisy football fans, prowled by surly policemen, the air made greasy by fried burgers from the van that parked on the corner. Beneath the sports-casually dressed, pot-bellied figures, chip wrappers and cigarette packets would litter the ground. It was a depressing image.

The House of Constant Shadow

He decided to retire to the back of the house. Movement caught his eye as he emerged into the garden. The strange man who lived opposite was seated at a table on his lawn, reading a newspaper. Ernest watched for a moment as a young woman came out of their back door carrying a plate of toast. She took a seat at the table and they chatted, although the distance was too far to make out the words. Ernest stood close to his own rose bushes, peering discreetly through the trellis that fringed the fence.

As he watched them, he slowly became aware of something curious about the couple, and the realisation crept upon him. The male looked to be in his early twenties, the girl a year or two younger. But close up, the proximity exposed something far more telling. His features looked remarkably like that of Ernest's, when he was of a similar age; that same angular jaw-line, slightly protruding ears, high cheekbones – even the neat sideburns and hairline lent the man an old-fashioned look. The young brunette was also unsettling, in the way she flicked her head back when she laughed, and the casual way she tucked her curls behind her ear. Whilst her hair was cut in the same recent style of modern women, her face shared a striking resemblance to that of Elsie; as she watched the man speak, she licked her lips with a recognisable intensity.

The House of Constant Shadow

Ernest was wrenched out of his reverie by a sudden stabbing pain in his stomach. He let out a gasp and staggered back, holding onto the back of a wooden bench for support. Rather than subsiding as he'd expected it to, the pain seemed to grip him in a prolonged throb, creating a sickening lurch of his vision. He stumbled along the garden path, blundering into the house. It felt as if his stomach was molten lava. He only just made it to the toilet in time. Afterwards, exhausted, he collapsed onto the bed as the gripes slowly abated.

Much later he awoke. The house was quiet. He gingerly climbed out of bed and went downstairs. Margaret was snoring in the armchair again. He drifted back out to the garden, tentatively pressing his stomach.

The couple from the house opposite had gone. He felt strangely relieved. Now Ernest was outside he could hear the clamour of the crowd from inside the football stadium; the voices were discordant and deep, imbued with threatening intent.

He busied himself with harvesting the rose hips that grew in the corner of the garden, collecting the vivid red fruits in a thin sandwich bag. The pestle and mortar in his shed would grind them into a fine powder once they were dried. They would come in useful.

The House of Constant Shadow

Days folded into each other. A period of warm weather swept in, leaving the house uncomfortable and throbbing. Ernest spent a lot of time at the window of the back bedroom, watching the couple opposite, fascinated by their resemblance to the youthful likenesses of him and Elsie. He even took several photographs with the camera, but when he cranked up the digital zoom to examine their faces the features just looked hazy and indistinct. Only his eyes detected that their movement was familiar.

A couple of days later someone poured paint-thinner on the untaxed Subaru that was parked at the back of the Farnhams' house. The following weekend Ernest discovered that his clematis had been hacked down.

The next wave of sickness occurred on the last Friday of the month. He'd been prowling the house, restless with frustration. A quick call to Crystal earlier had ignited his libido, and he was watching the clock. During the night he'd emptied the crushed rose hips into Margaret's underwear drawer. Her incessant scratching was keeping him amused. The room was stifling; humidity seemed to fester in the darkness. An aroma of sweat encircled her chair like a fog.

"Ernie, it must be that washing powder!" She displaced a huge breast as she scratched beneath its overhang. "You know how my skin's sensitive – it must have irritated me."

"Want me to run you a bath, dear?" His gentle tone was at odds with the delight that lit up his face.

"You'll have to. I'll never sleep tonight."

He thought about how much she slept in her armchair, snoring at the television or the radio. "Yes, dear, nothing worse than an irritation," he said as he ascended the stairs.

He'd just reached the top when the stomach cramps hit him again. This time he felt a quiver of ice in his belly, almost as if he'd swallowed a frozen bubble. As before, the grip of pain intensified. He crashed into the toilet.

This time there was evidence afterwards; the porcelain was spattered with blood, as well as everything else. The sight alone increased his queasiness. His stomach felt bloated and raw. Sleep was the only option for the next few hours. When he awoke later, he reluctantly called the doctor to make an appointment.

The next few weeks were a blaze of activity; doctors' visits and samples, shopping, and the general drudgeries of day to day life. It was fair to say that there was little time for Crystal, Eleanor and the Farnhams, let alone any opportunity for Ernest's games. Margaret remained ignorant of why things seemed to be continuing without the bad luck that sometimes dogged her; the snapped laces, the furniture banged into, the occasional bout of diarrhoea; it was too close to home for Ernest to slip her the usual laxative in her food. He was having enough problems that way himself.

One afternoon when he was trudging back from the supermarket, he spotted the couple who lived opposite washing their car. He stood for a moment, panting heavily in his thick coat, watching the man hose soap suds off the vehicle. The intensity of the man's movement - they were facets of his own that had been long forgotten. Ernest felt a surge of regret. Regret for what he'd once had, regret for what he'd once been, regret for what he'd since become.

He got his appointment for the doctor to discuss the biopsy results. The night before, he experienced an intense tangle of dreams. In his mind he was a boy again, playing in the fields of his uncle's farm. The late summer colours were as golden as he'd remembered. The sun was just as warm on his skin. The delight in his friends' faces was just as intense, as they capered carelessly in that idyllic childhood time.

The House of Constant Shadow

When he awoke that morning he was plunged back into his present state of existence; an immense form lagging next to him in bed; city traffic crawling noisily along the street outside; pale light filtered through threadbare curtains at the window. Decades of resentment separating what was then, from now.

The funny thing was, the dream had stirred memories of what his heart had once felt. It was a feeling that promised hope.

He made sure that Margaret had all she needed before he set out for the health centre. The dream seemed to have attached to his thoughts. It may just have been the sunshine and the birdsong that conjured childhood reminiscences, not the night-time visions, but it felt like he was yearning for a different mindset. He was tired of the *nastiness* of it. Seeing the young couple from opposite had just reinforced the futility of his current existence. So it was with a deep breath that Ernest left the comfort of the courtyard and went to see the doctor.

*   *

He stumbled through the doors of the shiny new health centre, dazzled by the technology and his own unfamiliarity of the building. A smell of paint clung to his coat from the interior's hand-rails. The bus rocked him all the way home. He stared unseeing through the window, balancing the implication of the news the doctor had just imparted.

Cancer.

Colours blazed with a renewed intensity as the bus passed. Senses roared in his head. He glanced down at the bulge of his stomach, imagining the mass of black cells that were multiplying in the time the bus waited at the traffic lights.

Cancer.

The world continued spinning on its axis as the realisation of his own mortality was born. Two minutes wasted by teenagers arguing with the driver were 120 seconds that seemed sickening in their triviality.

The finishing line was finally within sight. Rather than the end, Ernest viewed the coming months as a celebration of his endurance; a release from the game that had begun over 35 years before. The doctor had said he wouldn't see another Christmas, yet outside the trees were heavy with the weight of summer leaves, pedestrians strolled in t-shirts.

As he alighted the bus, the young man and woman from the house opposite were walking a dog in the park. He watched them embrace, not even registering the familiarity of their conduct, ignoring the recognisable aspect of their movement. Something was gestating inside now, something that had grabbed his attention and could not be halted by even the most powerful of distractions. The blackness within him felt malformed and grotesque.

Of course he told Margaret the news. He was surprised by the tenderness of her reaction. Her tears seemed genuine, barely without a trace of self-interest. The uncertainty of her own future - without his constant presence to care for her - was never once mentioned. Perhaps it hovered unspoken, banished by good taste and fearful subtlety. Perhaps she had spoken to a doctor separately, maybe someone had put her mind at rest. Perhaps she simply didn't care.

All he understood was his determination to enjoy the remaining months. There were many games that he'd planned over the years, many trials and cruelties that had been designed, squirreled away for the future. Well, that future was now.

In the house of perpetual darkness, Ernest sat in the chair, counting down the remaining time with each beat of his bitter heart.

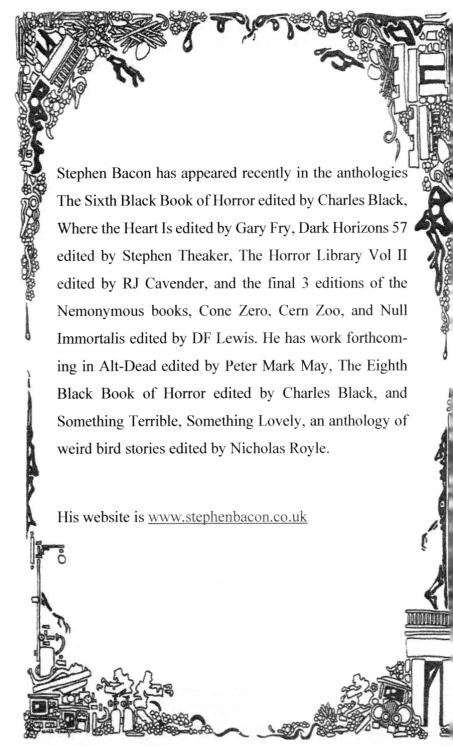

Stephen Bacon has appeared recently in the anthologies The Sixth Black Book of Horror edited by Charles Black, Where the Heart Is edited by Gary Fry, Dark Horizons 57 edited by Stephen Theaker, The Horror Library Vol II edited by RJ Cavender, and the final 3 editions of the Nemonymous books, Cone Zero, Cern Zoo, and Null Immortalis edited by DF Lewis. He has work forthcoming in Alt-Dead edited by Peter Mark May, The Eighth Black Book of Horror edited by Charles Black, and Something Terrible, Something Lovely, an anthology of weird bird stories edited by Nicholas Royle.

His website is www.stephenbacon.co.uk

The Rat Catcher's Apprentice

Ross Warren

It was a quiet night in the smoking room of the Carlton club. The stormy winds and heavy rains that had battered London for the best part of three days were keeping all but the most die-hard of patrons in their homes.

So it was that Charles Wentworth found himself sharing a late night tot of whiskey in front of the fire with Punch magazine editor Henry Mayhew. The two men sat either side of the large fireplace in well maintained leather settees of a rich mahogany colour, a pause in their conversation meant the only sound was the crackle and snap as the logs burnt in the hearth.

'So tell me Henry,' Charles said, leaning forward. 'What stories have you to tell from your time studying the poor and suchlike?'

'Well as you can probably imagine, you see the same things happening amongst the poor and destitute whichever part of London you care to venture into,' he took a large swallow of whiskey before continuing. 'Solace is taken in whatever they can find that closest resembles alcohol and violence and thievery are a daily occurrence.'

'It's to be expected amongst the lower class I suppose. You must have heard the odd interesting tale though?'

'Well, by far the most interesting of the characters I came across was a fellow by the name of Jack Black. Have you heard of him?'

'Ah yes, the Queen's Rat Catcher! By Jove I bet he was a strange chap indeed.'

'Quite! I spent several days with him and it was certainly an eye opener. The story I am about to relay to you must go no further than these walls, I have a reputation to uphold and this could be construed as quite a fanciful tale.' Mayhew reached forward to refill his tumbler and then on settling back began his tale.

****

I first saw Mr. Black, Rat and Mole destroyer to her majesty Queen Victoria, on the corner of Hart Street. He looked resplendent in his self-made 'uniform', comprised of a topcoat of the deepest scarlet, waistcoat, breeches and the most ornate of leather belts inset with cast-iron effigies of rats.

On this occasion he had a cart set up containing cages filled with rats. The cart itself was decorated with pictures of the vermin on the panels and the tailboard. Black was demonstrating to the gathered congregation of street urchins and barrow boys the potency and effects of his poison by placing some in the mouth of a light grey rat he was holding. We spoke briefly and agreed I should meet him the following day at his home in Battersea.

The rat catcher's parlour was more akin to a shop than a family abode, all about were boxes and cages containing all manner of rats, ferrets and birds. Along one wall was a work bench upon which lay animals at various stages of taxidermy. All around the room hung paper bags and I enquired of my host as to their contents.

'All of them Sir,' he said reaching to take one down to show me. 'Contain cured fish for eating.'

I declined his offer of a taste, but was wholehearted in my acceptance of the offer of a little morning tea before the day's tasks were to begin in earnest.

The Rat Catcher's Apprentice

Black's wife produced a pot of strong tea and some rock-like scones with out so much as a grunt of acknowledgment. A heavy-set woman with the disposition of a corpse, I got the distinct impression that simply rising from her chair marked this as an honoured visit. We were joined at the table by a boy of about fourteen who had the unruliest mass of red hair I had laid my gaze upon in many a year. His side of a brief conversation consisted of an assortment of inarticulate grunts and I took that as an indication that he was from Mrs Black's side of the family.

'And who might this young fellow be?' I enquired when their discussion had come to an end.

'This is my nephew Timothy. His Ma, my wife's Sister, has sent him to me in the hope that a spell as my apprentice will give him a bit of purpose,' Jack said with an evident lack of enthusiasm.

'So, you want to be a rat catcher do you?'

Before the boy could reply, with what I fully expected to be a mono-syllabic grunt, Jack had risen from the table and was readying himself to leave the house. Waistcoat fastened and satchel slung across his chest the Queen's rat catcher marched out of his house leaving the boy and I to scurry after him like rats following the pied piper.

The Rat Catcher's Apprentice

On the way to the first scheduled appointment of the day Jack explained to me how the actual work he undertook for her majesty only accounted for about ten percent of his annual workload but the prestige ensured he always had other work come his way. The majority of commissions came from the more affluent households of society such as the bankers, barristers and landowners.

So it was that our first stop was to a rat infestation in the wine cellar of a gentleman of some importance at Lloyds of London. As Jack skittered about the darkened cellar, lit as it was by a single gaslight scarcely up to the task, he explained the process to me.

'It's very rare to encounter any actual vermin in a location such as this, but there's plenty of their leavings to show activity.'

Jack seemed positively delighted to have an attentive person taking interest in his job. The so called 'apprentice' was showing little interest, preferring instead to pull bottles from the impressive wine racks and study the labels. I had no doubt that he lacked the ability to read what was written upon them.

'A job such as this is of the easiest sort,' Jack went on, seemingly oblivious to the abject lack of attention from his protégé.

'What, may I ask, are the toughest commissions?' The actions of the lad were beginning to irritate me but I tried not to show it to my amiable host.

'Any work in the sewers is the worst Sir. Working by a single gas light is tricky enough but then you have the smell and you encounter more of the little beasties.'

I left Jack to continue with his baiting and headed over to give his inattentive lad a stern talking to.

'Now hear this young man...' That was as much of my sermon as I was able to orate before a rat the size of a badger launched itself from the opening that Timothy had just extracted a fine cognac from. The creature emitted a high pitched shriek as it leapt upon the boy, fastening itself to his face. A muffled scream sounded from beneath the black hairy mass that covered his face like an animated balaclava.

I stood motionless for what seemed like minutes, but in reality was mere seconds, before making a futile attempt to remove the monstrosity from the boy as he writhed about the floor of the cellar. Just as I was starting to fear that the rat would gnaw Tim to death, Jack arrived on the scene. Using the wooden cudgel from his belt he beat the creature until it released its hold on the boy's ravaged face and tried to attack the rat catcher. Jack continued to batter the creature until it was little more than a pile of bloody flesh and matted hair.

I took off my tunic and pressed it to the pulped remains of the apprentice's face in an attempt to staunch the flow of blood. Between us we carried the boy back to Jack's house, where his wife set about tending the wounds.

Twenty minutes, and the best part of a bottle of medicinal alcohol, later the scale of the damage was apparent for us to see. Most of the boy's nose had been eaten away, one eye was a sightless gooey mess and there were two deep furrows on either cheek that required some crude stitching from Mrs Black. A multitude of additional bites and scratches covered his face, neck and shoulders with many already bruising yellow and blue around the edges. When Jack and I finished our appraisal of the damage Mrs Black wrapped the boy's head using a roll of bandage, leaving just the single working eye exposed. Its contracted pupil denoting that the boy remained in a state of shock. No doubt he had a bout of fever to look forward to as well.

At my forceful insistence it was agreed that I would accompany Jack for the remainder of the week. I would be able to garner further information for my articles whilst at the same time providing an extra pair of hands in place of the bed-ridden apprentice. I took Jack up on the offer of the guest room, saving me an early hour commute each day.

I awoke the following morning at, an early for me, seven o'clock and found the rat catcher already at the kitchen table eating a large bowl of porridge. Given his stoic expression I deduced that porridge making was not one of Mrs Black's skills and decided a cup of tea would suffice for my own breakfast.

'How's the boy today? I asked between sips of the scolding brew.

'The fever has its grip on him, so says the missus. She's going to change his dressings soon, we'll be able to asses the damage.'

The rest of our morning sustenance was taken in silence, broken six or seven minutes later by the creaking of a door. I must admit it gave me quite a start.

'You can see him now,' Mrs Black said when her head appeared around the edge of the door.

The room we entered was dimly lit as if any increase in illumination might cause the patient distress. From the doorway we could just make out the shape of the boy propped up in bed on two sturdy looking pillows. Mrs Black hovered on the far side of the boy's bed as if anxious to wrap his wounds and get them hidden from sight as quickly as possible.

The Rat Catcher's Apprentice

When Jack and I made it to the bedside we had gained some adjustment to the darkness and were able to see a face so ravaged it was difficult to reconcile it to the boy I had met the previous morning. I thank providence that my experiences over the two years prior had hardened my constitution; my younger self would have fled the room in search of a secluded place to empty the contents of my stomach post haste.

The deep wounds in each of the boy's cheeks had already scabbed over, leaving the skin bone white and wrinkled as if lacking moisture. His right eye was a knotted mess of lacerated flesh and sinew, white pus trickled from the ravaged socket and ran a course down his cheek like a canal on a map of Birmingham. I took this to be the fluid of his ruined eyeball and had to be strong-willed to suppress myself from gagging. However, by far the worst damage was centred in the middle of the boy's face where his nose had previously made its residence.

The pink, freckled flesh of the nose had all but been eaten away, bite marks and claw scratches were in evidence on the cheeks either side of the mess that remained. The cartilage of the nose had been pulled forward which coupled with the extensive swelling to the boy's mouth and lips gave the impression of a snout. More disturbing than the damage to the boy's features though was a collection of a dozen or so course ginger hairs that had sprouted up along the unscathed jaw-line. It was this image more than any other that failed to leave my mind during the following day's activities with Jack.

It was near dark when we returned from a day's work that had taken us as far as Islington. Any tiredness we might have been feeling was shocked from our system when we set eyes upon the devastation that had been unleashed on Mr Black's kitchen. The table was over-turned, one leg shattered into splinters. The contents of the larder were strewn about the flagstone floor, with many of the items looking half eaten. A block of butter had melted into a yellow pool which spread several feet into a second yellowish puddle that was most definitely not butter.

Amongst this sea of detritus sat Jack's wife, sobbing uncontrol-lably into a balled –up handkerchief. Jack crouched beside his wife and spent several minutes consoling her, getting her calm enough to ask her for an account of events.

'Little Timmy woke about three in the afternoon,' Mrs Black began before pausing to dab once more at her eyes. 'He was feverous and began screaming for food. I gave him some bread and pork that I had ready on the bedside table, but that weren't enough for him. He knocked me over in his hurry to get to the larder.'

'Where is the boy now dear?' Jack enquired, rising from his haunches. His distraught wife simply motioned in the direction of the boy's bedroom before once more burying her tear stained face in her sodden hankie.

We approached the room with trepidation, half expecting the boy to attack us and prepared if necessary to subdue him with physical force. Instead we found him sleeping peacefully with half-eaten, congealing food coating the blankets he slumbered beneath. Large strips of his bandages were mixed amongst the food revealing his hideously disfigured face. The swelling about his mouth and the remains of his nasal appendage had increased giving it an even more pronounced, snout-like appearance. Where there had been the dozen or so thick ginger hairs there was now the beginnings of a small beard giving the impression of fur along the chin. I put this worrying sight down to the poor lighting of the room and followed Jack to the bedside where we cleaned and redressed the sleeping child's wounds.

With our task satisfactorily completed we retired to the parlour where Jack produced a bottle of malt whiskey with which we settled our nerves in order to have some chance at a peaceful nights slumber when we retired for the evening. It wasn't the best quality of scotch but it did the trick! When we headed to our respective rooms the bottle was all but empty.

My alcohol assisted sleep was broken by sounds of a commotion coming from the ground floor of the property. I donned a housecoat and ventured to investigate. On exiting my room I came across Jack on the landing dressed in hastily fastened breeches and a half tucked-in night-shirt. We exchanged a brief word about the noise and together descended the stairs to the darkened floor below.

The kitchen was largely undisturbed with just the back door showing signs of damage. The lower panel was busted through from the inside. A closer inspection of the splintered hole in the door revealed a couple of small clumps of ginger fur snagged around the makeshift opening. The door into the boy's room stood ajar revealing a lit lantern upon the dresser that sat to the right of the door. Jack lit a lantern of his own and we entered the room. To my considerable relief it proved to be unoccupied and I let out an audible sigh. The bed clothes were in disarray and there was a vast pool of urine on the exposed mattress. The vanity mirror of the dresser was shattered and the lacquered surface of the dresser had been scratched with four deep, parallel grooves as if an animal had attacked it instead of a disorientated and scared little boy. The cause of his apparent anger and rage was revealed to us by the pile of soiled bandages that littered the floor.

****

Henry drained the last of the amber liquid from his tumbler and reclined into his seat.

'And thus concludes my little tale of mystery. You can see, I'm sure, why such fanciful events must not go beyond this room.'

'Of course, we all have reputations to maintain, but what became of the boy?'

'He was never heard from again,' Mayhew said rising from his chair and walking over to the hat stand that held his coat. 'Jack, myself and several local men spent the best part of two days searching, but to no avail'

Mayhew fastened his coat and wandered back across to where Charles remained seated.

The Rat Catcher's Apprentice

'There have been rumours and sightings of a giant ginger furred creature wandering Battersea at night. You know how these urban legends embellish the facts; Rat Boy at large indeed!'

Mayhew reached out and gave Charles a hearty handshake and bid him goodnight. Charles remained alone, finishing his own glass of whiskey and pondering the weird tale so recently regaled to him. A shiver worked its way through his body as a clap of thunder sounded out and the street visible though the window was illuminated by lightning. In the momentary brightness Charles thought he saw the bandaged face of a boy staring in through the window. Charles shook his head and placed his still half full glass upon the table before him.

'I think you've had quite enough for tonight Charles,' he said shrugging on his own coat and fastening it in readiness for braving the stormy streets for the two minute walk back to his own warm house.

As the door of the Carlton Club banged closed behind him a second clap of thunder rang out above his head, as it echoed between the houses either side of the street it sounded to him eerily like the pleading of a distraught man.

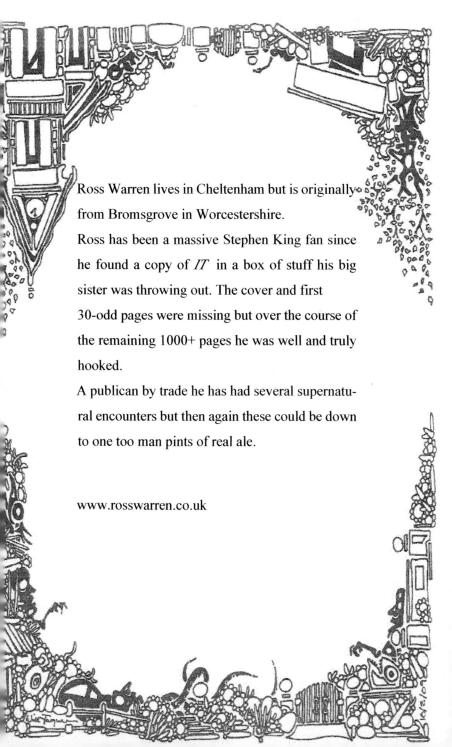

Ross Warren lives in Cheltenham but is originally from Bromsgrove in Worcestershire.

Ross has been a massive Stephen King fan since he found a copy of *IT* in a box of stuff his big sister was throwing out. The cover and first 30-odd pages were missing but over the course of the remaining 1000+ pages he was well and truly hooked.

A publican by trade he has had several supernatural encounters but then again these could be down to one too man pints of real ale.

www.rosswarren.co.uk

The Anchorite's Daughter

Shaun Hammel

1.

Fourteen years ago Ted and Glenda Eyerstone were married in Gatlinburg, Tennessee, in a small hideaway chapel, on the outskirts of that
famous mountain town. It was an elopement; they could not wait for
their planned date some three months later. And there were some less
dramatic, practical reasons as well. The honeymoon was spent alone in a
small cabin tucked high in the foothills, with a spa, a bar, a king-sized bed.
They didn't leave the cabin for three days. They still had their ceremony
later in the fall for friends and family, in a bigger church with an intri-
cately latticed multi-tiered cake, Celtic music strummed by a friend of the
bride who did it for free, massive explosions of hyacinth, peonies, and
blood-velvet roses, a proper minister, a lavish wedding dress, a teary-
eyed father either glad to finally be giving her away or simply overcome
by the moment. This day was beautiful, moving and made Glenda very
happy and Ted very relieved when it was finally over. But they had that
secret between them: they were already married. Privately, they enjoyed

this special knowledge that only the two of them knew, and Glenda hoped no one else would find out about for the rest of their lives. No one ever did. (A secret sunk is a secret well-kept).

Ted stood on the balcony of their 12th story apartment, looking down at the city sparkling many-colored jewels in the night. His wife was inside on the sofa-- now a good thirty pounds heavier than the day they were married-- pretending to read a magazine, a Cosmopolitan, or Vogue. She was working on her fifth glass of wine and he was well into his third Brass Monkey. A light tinkling of anonymous jazz played on the stereo. Ted introduced her Miles Davis, John Coltrane, Charlie Parker, and others, early on in their marriage, but somehow only the most platitudinous, non-confrontational jazz appealed to her. And now that's all she listened to, almost out of spite, Ted thought. They had just returned from a dinner celebrating the retirement of one of her bosses at the CarpetWorld marketing firm she had worked for all these years. He could smell the leftover scent of her perfume, something bottom-heavy from the Amber family, still clinging to his nostrils, like a lingering snide remark. He was a chemist who worked for a small local perfumery, and it was "his bag"-- as Glenda liked to blurt out. She never bought or used any of the perfumes he created for the company, or any of the other companies he'd worked for during in the past fourteen years. He stopped giving them as gifts to her early on in their marriage. But she loved to tell the world he invented perfumes for a living.

It was something she had said, of course. Wasn't it always? One of her co-workers, some alcoholic swooning salesman named Rex, had leaned his rosy snout well into Glenda's cleavage and took a deep snort, then commented something banal about her "enticing odor". *She reeked like a dead tree slathered in cinnamon oil! Get it right, jerk!* But no, Ted was his usual subdued, passive self and downed drink after drink, shriveling up a bit more with each one.

When one of the office girls, Sheila Something, blurted out drunkly at him, "Why are you so quiet Ted!" he nearly sprang from his coiled rattlesnake position and hurled himself clear over the table, through the gathering storm of cigarette and cigar smoke and residue of office gossip and bolts of shrieking laughter like lightning, to clutch both hands around her tiny neck, squeezing hard, too hard and fast and bloodlusty for anyone to prevent her certain death. It was a question he heard every time he went out with his wife and after years of stuttering out lame explanations-- "I'm a happy-go-lucky introvert!", "Well, you know, I'm a scientist by nature, and chemist by profession, and our types tend to sit back and observe the world..."-- he finally came to the conclusion a pale polite smile and bobbing of the head was the best response. At the time Ted was not doing so well with his company, and his salary and commission had been cut dramatically. When a waiter passed by, Glenda patted the boy on his ass and said for all to hear, "If my husband had an ass this tight, I wouldn't care if I had to pay all the bills!" They all turned and looked at him, . "Haha, dear." A nebular thought even then, beginning to form in his head.

The Anchorite's Daughter

Within a week his company regretted to inform him that they were no longer in need of his services. They wanted to go with a newer, fresher team. Team? He was the only one getting the ax!

"You know the game, Ted," his immediate boss, Franklin Invernes, was saying as Ted packed away his supplies, "The owners just don't understand that inspiration for new and appealing colognes is not something that can be cornered, defined and put on a deadline... you're a good guy, Ted, a talented guy, Ted, and you've made this company more money than Speikermann even realizes..." Then Franklin, a vacuum of forget already forming, ceased to speak. He looked like a taxidermist's rendition of his former friend and boss.

As he carried his box through the maze of hallways to the elevator, Grigory Vintii, one of the company's salesmen and happy-hour comedians, came out of a glass door leading to the graphics department and patted him on the back. Vintii had made a small fortune last year off Ted's line of curry-chutney, and other Indian cuisine-themed perfumes, with a top note of applescent and a fougere base.

"Say, old sport, you're not going to come back with a load of guns in your trenchcoat and blast up the joint, are ya old pal.. heh heh..."

"I don't own a trench coat."

Then Vintii's sun set suddenly, going blue-dark morose. "Hey, Teddo, you know I'm just kidding with ya? Good luck and all."

The Anchorite's Daughter

Out on Broad Street he felt underwater, and the box of chemical supplies and personal items weighed in his arms like a ship's anchor. Steamy August clouds lazed overhead. A bus-- not his-- zoomed by too close to the curb, and he felt the rush of air from it like a whitecap. Although it went by at thirty or more miles per hour he saw, or thought he saw, every face on the right side of the bus, and they all had blackened, dead eyes, drooping mouths, disheveled hermit hair. The hot sun poured down on him like lava. Everything, buildings, cars, people, benches and bus kiosks, seemed to sway like submerged vegetal matter. He began to walk slowly south toward the river. A homeless black man carrying, of all things, a broom, sat up against grafitted wall of an abandoned shopfront and smiled toothlessly at him. Ted went over to him and dropped the box. "Want to trade?" A look of incredulity flashed in his bloodshot eyes. "You want my broom, bossman? What you got in there?" He looked into the box, studying the items, not really grasping their meaning. "What am I gonna sweep off the concrete with when I lay down tonight?" But it was obvious to Ted the man wanted these strange vials and containers and folders more than he wanted the broom. "Here, take it."

As Ted began to walk off with the broom, the black man said, "Hey, white boy, what you want with that broom anyhow?"

2.

After walking several blocks, his bones like swamp water, Ted noticed a young woman sitting alone at a bus kiosk. He decided to sit on the bench beside, careful not to invade her sphere of comfort. He would not classify her as exactly beautiful, but her large and luminous eyes were intriguing, and her straight black hair cut abruptly just above the shoulders appealing. She wore an orange leopard-patterned blouse with thin straps instead of sleeves and tight black leather pants. Her body gave the impression of a long slender candle misshapen over the years with globs of redistributed wax. But her face was young. She was no more than twenty-five. When she turned her head to see who sat down near her, she didn't flash away shyly, like most people would, but her gaze seemed to linger uncritically upon him. Perhaps even a slight smile cracked, after taking notice of the broom which rested between his legs. Then quite surprisingly she said something.

"Are you the kiosk keeper?"

"Hmm? Oh-- this?" He squeezed the handle tightly with his left hand. "It's a present for my wife."

The girl scratched her cheek and waved away a fly from her face. He noticed part of a tattoo showing on her right breast. She had a pair of shades saddled on her thigh. She put them on.

"Well, here's my bus, catch ya--Hope your wife doesn't fly the coop." She boarded the bus and Ted watched as her strange lumbering gait took her all the way to the rear of the bus. Not once did she look his way.

He walked the entire three miles to his apartment building across the river. Halfway across the pedestrian bridge he stood and watched some guy do an epileptic dance. He was wearing really tight blue shorts and a cut-off T-shirt, and sandles on his feet. A baseball cap lay on the ground, apparently there to accept coin from interested onlookers. Past him, the river curled toward Wolf Shoe Bend-- where a mental hospital had been built on top of sacred Cherokee burial land-- its gray-brown water blending finally into the hazy hills. Asocial cumulus clouds hung heavily in the sky, unwilling to consort with their fellow cloud-brothers and form a refreshing afternoon thunderstorm. The nut job's rain dance wasn't working.

By the time Ted reached his apartment, he was hot, humid and angry. It finally sunk in properly. The bastards had fired him! Surprisingly, he found his wife home early from work. She was stirring up a drink a their small pullaway bar underneath the blank wall where the large original Hallfleece painting used to be. He remembered his wife's expression of revulsion when the delivery men brought it to the apartment (its dimensions were 9' by 6') and unwrapped it from its brown paper covering. "What...in..the. That's hideous!"

"I thought you'd like it Glenda."

"It looks like a poorly drawn monk being flushed down a giant toilet bowl! The colors are so bland and brown and uninspiring. It makes me wanna hurl!"

"I believe that was the artist's intent, Glenda. Why does it always feel like we're in an Edward Albee play?"

"Huh?"

The Anchorite's Daughter
****

Yes, Ted thought, if only their conversations could be like they once were, so literate, so piquant, so arousing. He realized his shirt was soaked in sweat.

"Hi, honey." He held the broom bristles-side up, like the farmer's pitchfork in that famous painting, *American Gothic*.

Glenda nearly spilt her drink, laughing suddenly, violently. "You haven't called me 'honey' in fourteen years of marriage, Ted! What have you turned jokester all of a sudden. Brushing up for open mike night down at the Happy Nugget? What the fuck do you have there, Ted!" She giggled nervously.

"Oh, Glenda, sorry. I almost forgot our anniversary. I got this for you..."

"Ted, you're an idiot. Our anniversary isn't for three months," she blurted, then something distant, like the sun visible from Neptune, dawned on her. "Oh." "Well that's just lovely, Ted. A fucking broom."

"No, dear. I just remembered. Suddenly. Had to grab the first thing I saw you might like. Knowing your fashionable and eclectic tastes... Well, I thought about bringing the owner of this broom instead for dinner. But I fear he couldn't chew the food you normally prepare.."

"Ok, ass. Why are you home, it's early." She took down her drink in one gulp.

3.

It was morning in the summer mountains, but Wilson Greer was already beginning to sweat. And like most mornings these days, he felt his heart skip around in his chest with those increasingly strange beats. He leaned on his walking stick, light-headed. He thought, irrationally, that if he bent over to pick up a curious pebble, or spy the morning routine of dung beetle, he would die. But the dizzying palpitations stopped just as quickly as they came on, and he felt alright again. Stream became unhindered by boulder, river to dreaming ocean, blood flowed to greater blood. In the midst of his having to leave, thoughts of his daughter flooded back-- how many daughters of the forest had he ad-opted in an effort to forget the real one? Who knows. Memories always bled back from the sleeping oceanic past to disturb his hermitage. There was nothing to do to combat it, he had decided years ago, so he simply just got on with his day.

He didn't want to leave his home of over a decade, but the new road paved through the mountains had brought tourists, more hunters, poachers, adventurous city-dwellers, fat older couples on motorbikes and also, more ranger presence. They were running him off finally (for all these years they knew he was here and cast a blind eye, but now they were going to pave the dirt jeep trail that wound its way around Old Smokestack mountain; he even had a few terse exchanges with Tucker

The Anchorite's Daughter

McKinlin, a stern-faced ranger whose wife died of cancer when she was only thirty-five). Twelve beautiful years of isolation dissolved so sweetly into memory, were now coming to an end. His eyes pointed down and focused on one random spot on Cutler's Mountain, thought perhaps he saw a trickle of water. There probably wasn't a forest service road to get his truck anywhere near there. He could never find it anyways. Once under the canopy he'd lose track of the spot; he would never find that exact location, no matter how many times he bore it into memory.

The day he left his church, his wife, his daughter, he did not leave behind his religion. It was just as real-- heavier in fact-- than the materials he hauled up in his truck to build his hideaway home. Only difference was-- and it was a big difference-- that now he preached to the trees, to the rocks, to the rushing water. Sometimes a squirrel paid his sermons a moment of respect, before suddenly remembering a more promising nut to crack.

He headed back to his shack, made of river rock and poplar planks, with a roof built with swiped sections of corrugated steel siding from an abandoned warehouse down in Knoxville. Beside the shack was his faded green rusty Ford pick-up truck that he rarely drove anymore, with a tattered blue tarp thrown over the bed. He kept canned goods and other supplies there. He felt sweat streaming down his chin under his ratty gray-brown beard and under his cap. It was hot here, even at four thousand feet up, probably as high as 80 degrees. But in his chair in the shade underneath a slope-stunted beech tree, he would cool off quickly, catch a cooling breeze, maybe slide into a noon-time dream.

The Anchorite's Daughter

He hoped it wouldn't be like the last one. That one was too much pain. In the dream Wilson had decided to trim up his beard, get a haircut, put on a nice cheap suit and go visit his daughter in Sevierville. He expected to be greeted warmly by first the old hound in the yard, then a flock of happy screaming grandchildren, his ex-wife, Almira, rocking serenely, but with a slightly sardonic smirk, in the chair on the porch, then finally, by Julia, his daughter. But those expectations were not met. The hound barked and snapped viciously from the tight end of his chain, a brood of dirt-faced children stood expressionless in the yard. Then as he got closer they watched him, their eyes filling with dark expression, the younger ones with suspicion, the older ones with menace, and the old lady in the rocking chair spat tobacco out at his shiny boots in lieu of a greeting as he stepped onto the porch. "You don't belong here. You never did." Then Julia came out on the porch, wearing a flowing yellow dress and a white sunhat. But her hands were raw and calloused and big like a man's. She was holding a rifle crosswise in her hands. That had been his daddy's rifle, and those were his daddy's hands...

As he sat in his chair, occasionally flicking at blackflies, he wondered what would happen if he really did go down in the valley and visit his daughter. It was six months ago, that he drove by the double-wide trailer she and her mother and his four grandchildren lived in. He saw a tall bearded man with a baseball cap smoking a cigarette on the built-on porch, talking to another shirtless man sitting on an uprighted stump. Probably another boyfriend, or for all he knew, her husband. Wilson only drove by once or twice a year, and this was the first time he'd seen this man. Each time he came down out of the mountains to drive by his daughter's place, it was a different vignette, a clouded window, into the that life he left behind. He would also, invariably, drive by his old chapel where he used to perform impromptu weddings for tourists, but also where he gave sermons on Wednesdays and Sundays. He had only a small following, less than twenty members, and he often wondered if all had been assimilated by other churches, or did one or two lose their faith and backslide because of his sudden, inexplicable dissappearance. For the longest time, he fantasized that some of his flock would search him down and try to convince him to come back to the world, where his message was sorely needed. But no one ever came.

Off to the northwest he saw over the valley thunderstorms growing, merging, into one great supercell front. There would be rain and wild lightning this afternoon. The worst were those storms that skipped the valley entirely and formed directly in the upslope of the hills. Those storms came on with a supernatural abruptness, swallowed the mountain whole, turning all of Old Smokestack Ridge into a plasma lamp of sorts. Weird greens and blues, then up through the purples, reds and oranges as the sun broke back through the clouds. After, the forest would drip for hours, and that sound always had a purring effect on his soul. Distant thunder falling echoing away on the other side of the range, the storm tattered and defeated for the moment, only to gain momentum once again rising to meet the next ancient range to the west, deeper into North Carolina. The pungent rot of dead wood and understory would surround him like a warm breast, and he would sleep then, settled or unsettled, until early evening. In the almost dark he would start a fire and heat up a can of beans and have some stale crackers and a ripe tomato to go with it.

But now the sun baked over the small garden he kept and the gloom stayed over Knoxville. He was fond of imagining one of those storms over Knoxville one day simply taking away the whole town, leaving behind nothing but bare ground, no remnant of civilization. Just fertile red dirt to be reborn again. Maybe the storm would die off before hitting the mountains. That happened sometimes.

He slipped into a dream that had more truth in it than most dreams. He was still living in his old home near Gatlinburg and he walked in from church service to find his young daughter and still youthful wife, together, pleasuring a strange man while he sat in his recliner. The man had a shaved head, but long angular goatee, a tattoo of a pentagram on his left shoulder, and one of a dancing skeleton in tophat on his right forearm. His arms were crossed but there were other strange markings on his chest as well. A deeply disturbing stench filled the room, his nostrils, his brain, like an atomic cloud bursting.. a cross between incense, corpsereek and animal dung. Julia and Almira, both pulling their mouths off the stranger's organ at the same time, looked startled at first, then both began to smirk and laugh at him. Almira spoke: "You're home early, dear..." Then right before his eyes, the two women embraced and twisted into each other like writhing snakes, face going into face, chest merging into chest, until there was only one woman left. On her forehead was a small hole dripping blood and her eyes were sparkling ruby.

It was a woman he seemed to both know and not know. She pointed at him with her left hand, then she said, "Join us, my husband, my father. It is pleasure you can not even imagine..." She reached for a butcher's knife that was on the coffee table.

In the background the dark man, now robed in black said, *"Look close, Will's son, into the eyes of the fly."*

Wilson jolted awake and nearly fell out of his chair under the stunted beech tree. He was drenched in sweat by the nightmare. The sun was covered by the almost-living swarming clouds. He could see rain was imminent, as sheets were folded into sheets down into the hollow he called White's Cove. The wind, like a great hissing of flies, disturbed the canopy above him. Thunder, a stroke on the brain, rattled bones of memories there.

"O Lord, I should of done the deed. Forgive me...."

4.

September came and went and Ted could not help but notice the relief in his wife's eyes, that their marriage was falling apart. She was nearly always gone, staying overnight with Rex the Ridiculous, he was certain, and he was surprised how little he cared. He felt reborn, not in light, but in darkness.

With wide-open and new eyes, he took to walking the night streets...

On the first night, he saw the homeless man whom he had exchanged his work supplies for that broom (which still leaned on the foyer wall). He was with some stringy man with long unwashed hair, rows of dilapidated teeth and a ragged Pantera T-shirt. They both smelled like musk and swamp gas. The old black man didn't seem to recognize him, but the haggard metalhead smiled blackly, and said, "Give us a couple bones my man. We're like hungry you know." Ted passed on silently.

"Hey, hey! That's the white boy took my broom!" the black man said.

Ted kept walking, faster now, but soon felt a strong hand grab his shoulder. He turned and saw it was the black man now. Recognition was flashing in his bloodshot eyes. "Gimme my broom back, boss." A hideous tubercular cough-laugh followed.

Clicks slid up to Ted. "Lamar here says you stole his broom. I suggest you return it to us. Or-- or... give us a couple twenties. We can call it even".

Lamar looked skeptical. "Naw, I wants my broom, cuz. It belonged to my crackwhore ole lady and she's sho nuff the wicked witch of the west! Ain't that so, Clicks?"

Clicks stood with his arms crossed over his chest, nodding in agreement. "That bitch cast spells. Hey, righteous man, give us some bread."

94

The Anchorite's Daughter

Ted fumbled through his wallet and gave the men everything green he could find, a total of maybe seventy dollars. "I'll bring the broom back too. Here take this. I just got to get going." He was caught in that uncertain space between being mugged and just offering charity to some disenfranchised individuals. It was a most unpleasant space to be in.

They took the money and headed off in the opposite direction, probably to get a cheeseburger.

On the second night, he avoided Malcom X Avenue, where he'd been accosted by Clicks and Lamar and stayed on Vinecourt Blvd, which was trendier and catered to the local university crowd. There were plenty of late-night restaurants, bars and local music venues, drunken, sputtering college girls ambling along the sidewalks or in the street. One girl was holding the neck of a small crape myrtle outside a crowded beer joint. As he passed her he looked into the place and noticed the girl from the bus kiosk weeks ago, sitting at the bar, staring into a half-empty mug of Killian's Red. Her hair was mussed as if she just woke up and didn't bother to brush it down.

"Say, dude. I know you." It was the girl who had been puking into the large potted tree.

"I don't think so."

"As if, dude. My big bro is the bartender here. You're not with the pigs, are you? Because if you are, I'm twenty-one, AND A HALF!" She laughed as if this was the funniest joke in the world.

"Not a cop no, and if you will excuse me..."

Ted started inside, but the girl grabbed him by the shoulder. Second time in two nights some strange night crawler had handled him this way. This time he was angry.

"Please don't grab me like that, Miss." He suddenly realized he was holding tightly the girl's forearm. She jerked it away. He noticed red finger-shaped marks where his hand had been.

Her eyes were climbing up through viscous layers impetuous charm and novice civility. "Oww. I don't like your tone, Mister. Buy us a drink, doll face." Simple, lusted over charm was back, in the blink of an eye. *In other times, in other places...*

But here and now, he simply said, "No."

He walked on, toward the Garden of Vines and the Debutt's Museum of Southern Railroads. From there he could see the river, black silk with silver streamers of moonlight, and the vestiges of the Tennessee River Rail Bridge. It was the oldest bridge to cross the river within the city limits. A vertical lift bridge that he hadn't seen "lift" for barge traffic in his lifetime, he had always been fascinated by those houses that sat atop each lift tower. He imagined all sorts of cranks, massive pulleys, cog-works and squealing metal sounds up there. When he was a boy he used to think evil shadow creatures lived there, slept undisturbed and comforted by the horrific banshee winds. The bridge was a relic, rusted over, but still functioning. It still surprised him it had not been razed or rebuilt to modern codes. But he reasoned since it was only for rail traffic,

Norfolk-Southern was a bit less strict in following safety codes or the aesthetic principles of your typical urban beautification society. Ted was one who found it alluring, even beautiful, even in its present worn-down state.

On the third night, he noticed the broom missing. A muggy September wind blew in from the patio. Apparently his wife forgot to shut the sliding glass door before she took off to fuck Rex the Reticulator once again.

On the fourth and fifth nights he decided to stay in and see if his wife would show up. She never did. He stayed drunk. In his closet laboratory, he fiddled with pine extract, antelope musk and his wife's orgasmal fluids. She had been a good sport from time to time, got to admit it to yourself, Ted ole boy...

On the sixth night he considered filing a police report, but decided against it. He broke down and called her cell phone. It went straight to voice mail. All he could bring himself to say was, "Hi, honey, dinner's ready." The ding of the microwave soon after verified this statement.

It really pissed him off-- for reasons he could not quite pin down-- that Glenda had taken, thrown out, or flown out on, his broom. The last possibility amused him, sourly. He went out to his balcony and stared out over the river, and to the left, way in the distance, the Tenn-Bridge. Something odd made his eyes double-back. Hmm, that's strange. He'd never seen a light on in any of those weird high houses on the lift towers before. And even more strangely-- surely an ocular illusion-- the lights flickered as if the illumination was not electric but fire.

On the seventh night he found her, the girl from the bus kiosk over a month ago, on the day he got fired. She was sitting outside a small coffee shop on Vinecourt, on metal patio furniture sipping a a steaming mug of coffee. He was about to pass on, but she called him back.

"Hey, there again. The kiosk keeper right?" When he turned to look at her, a peculiar sultry smile lit up her face.

He grabbed a coffee and joined her and they talked all night. Ted about his job and hobby creating original perfumes and the girl, Jolina, about her dead-end soul-crushing job at a shoe store call center and about her dabblings in the occult. She told him about her friends who wanted her join their pagan group, The Cult of the Blue Herons, but how she found it all so frivolous and unconvincing and downright silly at times. She humored them occasionally, and attended their meetings and parties, but she always held back when they suggested she take the initiation rites. She was intrigued about Ted's occupation and most of the night was spent asking him tedious questions about the process and classification and experimentation of perfume making. Ted wholeheartedly obliged. They agreed to meet on the following night at the same cafe, around the same time. She asked, in a cute, innocent tone, if Ted would surprise her with a new scent. Ted said he would most certainly. They parted with an awkward handshake and Jolina's ambiguous deep sea smile.

On the eighth, nineth and tenth nights... No sign of the girl. And Ted's despair. Ted's emptiness. Ted's rage.

5.

Laughter like thunder made the rafters of the chapel vibrate, threatened to bring the whole worn-out building down. Then silence filled the room, the screaming of a baby subsiding as some dreamy-eyed woman held it under water too long. Candle light caused long wire-thin shadows to flicker against the flaking walls. Someone grafitti artist had painted the words, "Love Light Lester", on one of the walls in lurid red. Bubbles rose to the top of the greenish tank, and then finally, a stillness. The woman with strawberry hair, let the lifeless child sink to the bottom. She was completely naked. She began to massage her breasts and flick her tongue like a snake.

Down below, hooded figures knelt on both knees in a semi-circle around a tall man covered with tattoos. He held, both hands gripping, a glinting dagger out from his abdomen and pointed it at each member, and spoke some words, the same each time. "Sine ullo desiderio vive et ama." Candle-scent and feces mocked the air.

The floor of the abandoned chapel was littered with dust and broken glass and assorted litter. Every window, blasting loud black night, had panes of jagged anarchal glass.

The tall man, also naked, spoke again: "And someone else tonight must die."

Almost before he finished, his hooded disciples hissed loud whispers in chorus, "Pick me, pick me, pick me...." Chaotic shadow-fire danced across empty pews.

Their leader laughed. "No dipshits! We must kill a pig tonight! Some fat cow and her vapid mercantile whore of a lover!..." He tugged at his goatee, irritatedly.

Then up to the tranced and still writhing woman, "Julia, love, wake up. Please take the thing from the waters and bury it in the forest. Remember, six feet down!"

The woman's eyes suddenly caught candlelight, flickered demurely, and she smiled. She reached down with one arm and grabbed the lifeless infant by its arm and pulled it above the surface of the water. It had been a boy child. Its parts flopped wildly as she yanked it and smothered it not unlovingly in her arms. She slipped beyond the red velvet curtains backing the baptismal alcove. The green dead waters slurped gently, then rested, quiet for now.

*****

Outside the chapel, Wilson Greer sat in his idling truck, wondering what was going on inside his former house of worship. He turned his headlights off, and waited, watching through the side windows a concerto of flickering lights, expecting the whole place to go ablaze any moment, but it did not. He was certain he saw Julia among those who had entered over two hours ago.

The Anchorite's Daughter

A Knoxville station, through intermittent static, bleated out some Dolly Parton song, then after that, something way too old and sticky, by George Jones. He thought about walking up to one of the lower windows and seeing what was going on inside, but he stopped himself every time the desire to crept back up. After about an hour of watching, the lights inside went out. Soon after, dark figures sifted outside the side entrance, like jets of smoke. They all headed for the rear of the building. Minutes later a beatup van grinded through the gravel parking lot and headed south on the highway. Wilson waited another thirty seconds or so and pulled out slowly from his partially hidden location in a lot across the street and followed the van at a comfortable distance. In his rearview mirror he noticed a sudden explosion of incarnadine violence, bloodfire and wildsmoke, rapture and tumult, then all was lost as he took a sharp curve away from the city and bent toward the adumbrate foothills of the Smoky Mountains. He lost the radio station completely and clicked off the sudden blast of senseless static. For a long time after, still following the van south and south, his mind echoed the static, memories thoroughly dissolved now into nothingness. Nothingness night black and unloving like a dead lover back.

South and south, road bending back and forth, up and down, a drugged orgasmic woman writhing beneath him. Love was a circle through the black. Night clouds ate through hills of dead October. Love was a circle of fire etched upon the black veins of night-trees slacked.

A memory blazed suddenly, of Julia underneath a massive and mostly dead oak tree many many falls ago. She was eight or nine. The tree looked split halfway down the middle, as if from some giant's axe, and a blackened streak remained from a long forgotten lightning strike.

101

The Anchorite's Daughter

There were copper and gold tones in the October sunset, turning Julia's blonde hair into twines of firesnake. But what he remembered most was her face. Did his imagination create this face, or was the memory true? He could not rightly say. But her expression was not befitting a child; there was dark wisdom, even lust, in her eyes. And a smile betraying too much knowledge, too many layers of regret and empty passion, red and redolent eyes. Scent of dead burning leaves, womanmusk. And in him growing again, unnatural, unwanted, evil desire. "No! No! No!" he shouted then, and even now. Even now as the secret, dead and withered, tossed around like windblown oak moss in the sepulchre of his brain. Thoughts we drink to drown or allow suddenly, almost without meditation, to fly away on broomsticks into star-scarred october nights, to pollinate the world of nightmares, stitch the masks of the prematurely dead, these empty children breathing beneath with no life, no heart, into slumbering ears the secrets of the eternally darkened life. "No!" Again he shouted as his daughter reached down and plucked a maggot from the trunk of the tree. Smiling she placed it in her mouth, and chewed slowly, deliberately, vilely, savoring its sour spongy death....

*****

Spike, the tall one, the bearded one, the one driving, knew all along he was being tailed. Julia had spotted him even before they made it to the old abandoned wedding chapel on Codsack's Cove drive.

"Will he follow us all the way to the High Sanctuary of the Blue Herons?" Julia, sitting in the passenger seat, her face rigid and alternating long slow notes of dark with short blares of silvery light from oncoming headlights, barely opened her lips, saying, "He would follow me to Hell, and try to convert The Great Silent One himself. Stupid fuck."

They drove south and south, getting high on hellstench and hillshine. For forty miles, Spike manipulated Julia's clit while the rest of the coven writhed languorous and bewitched in the back of the van, bodies merging into one many-legged thing, an orgasmic caterpillar. Merging was something grander than Love, a magical lava flow of desire, from volcanoes of lust and murder.

One day the anti-rapture of will come, when stinking skeletons with hanging bits of rotted meat gather in city centers, godwhores and motherfuckers encircled and humping the empty spaces between bones, flickering twig-like remnants of tongues dancing around bonfires and fountains filled with shit-clumped sewer water. Then whole hives break off to roam the countryside for living survivors, humping with bones sharp as swords any fleeing warm-blooded thing. Screams of terror and pain quickly sublimating into moans of intense orgasm. Great gouts of green-tinted cum shower the country-side, sliming the trees, the abandoned buildings, monuments of a dead society. Earth becoming a sick green sun, pulsing erotic seas of mucus-- an orb of sickness palpitating infinite and divine. Miles-long black caterpillars swimming forever, rising to the surface to spout out lakes of catarrh sulphuric phlegm into a bloated atmosphere. Broken from its orbit now, it flies like a witless bomb through galaxies growing more massive with each aeon, each parsec, scouring green hell across the universe.

*****

The Anchorite's Daughter

And on the twelfth night, devil's night, eve to all hallows' eve,

Ted concocted a scent that sent him into dizzying hallucinations. Just playing around with odd ingredients, by accident really. One whiff, and he was gone. Storms of fire and duststorms of glass across a red-tinted venetian landscape, crossing burning dune after dune. Exoskeletons of strange arthropods carpeted the ground. Flame geysers sprayed from the holes dotting the bleakscape like gopher holes in hell.

6.

Lamar was finishing the last of the bottle of vodka, while Clicks stood on the bank, one foot higher and resting on a huge river boulder, an unwitting caricature of John Ross himself. Lamar was sprawled out on the bench thinking about Halloweens past, when he was a kid in the ghetto. One time his older brother was the ghost of Robert Johnson and he was dressed up as the devil. A four foot ten inch red-faced devil with horns made of aluminum foil. He wore a black tuxedo his mother had bought him for his Uncle Sherman's wedding, who one year later was shot by cops during a break-in of a pawn shop. They went down to the crossroads, brought smiles to a couple street girls and pushers and brought home sacks full of candy. At that moment, it seemed like the only truly wonderful moment in his entire life.

"Yo, Lamar! Check that out!" He was pointing down the pathway, deep in greenish shadows. A man was strolling their way. He looked drugged. Wavering as he walked, his head rolled around slowly on his neck.

Lamar saw, and made an immediate identification of the man. It was that guy who had swiped his broom.

Clicks was heading straight to the man. "Hey friend.. Beautiful night isn't it." Lamar tossed the empty bottle and walked over. They both faced Ted, who seemed barely conscious, and certainly didn't realize two men were accosting him. He walked right through them, hard-shouldering them out of the way. Lamar and Clicks looked at each other, stunned.

"Did you see his eyes! What was it he said?"

Jolina.

*****

Moon-haunted clouds peeled away finally from the Railway Bridge. Keeping their distance, Lamar and Clicks followed Ted as he made his way to the edge of the riverfront park and onto the embankment that rose to meet the tracks. They looked up and saw a great flickering of lights, definitely fire, inside one of the structures atop a lift tower. And what appeared to be dark bodies flowing against it, in mad shadow dances. "Looks like he's going up there," Clicks whispered.

*****

Massive cogwork, chains and pulleys were idle inside a room bursting with the light of a central bonfire. Against the walls shadows stretched, retracted, writhed and connected into chaotic patterns, completely unmathematical and wild. The heat was magnificent. The stench was of burning death.

The Anchorite's Daughter

Spike and the others tossed brooms onto the fire to quench its thirst, its eternal thirst. Piles of brooms of various head shapes and handle lengths littered the room in piles. All twelve were naked and greased with pig lard and their own mingled sweat. At times it appeared whole bodies merged into and out of each other. Julia into Michael, Michael in Orlene, Jake into Donna, Julia in Glenda. Only Spike stayed distinct and whole the entire time. He did not dance with the others. He waited. He could smell the coming of the infernal scent, the one he had longed for since discovering his love for maggots on his thirteenth birthday. He ate a mouthful of maggots and made love in them in his dreams. "He's near, my empty children!"

*****

Ted, with a thousand red eyes, the eyes of flies, walked along the tracks towards the lift tower. Great Blue Herons, lined on each side of him, were silent and still, twinkling like dark jewels, onxy, sapphire.

Once he reached the tower he opened the gate whose lock and chain lay busted on the ground. He climbed up the steep and narrow stairs that doubled back in an edged spiral all the way to the landing where the house sat. When he made the landing he peered into the one of the windows then pulled out the vial of perfume had had concocted earlier. He took one whiff and his eyes brightened and pulsed red to sun-red. He tossed the vial into the High House of the Blue Herons and had no time to escape the explosion, but he did not scream with the rest before burning parts, arms, legs, heads with hair of fire, arched out away from the bridge and went hurling, smoking, blackening, into the Tennessee.

*****

"Holy fuck!" Lamar shouted. Both Lamar and Clicks took off running down the long track they had come from, ears ringing with the explosion, and when they slide and tumbled down the embankment and realized they were in the clear, they stopped and looked up at the lift bridge. "What in the great goddamn is that?"

They saw a huge fly-like creature flying out of the hanging moon-glinted smoke and soot. They saw, as it approached, it's gleaming red eyes. Then as the creature flew low through the ornamental trees and just above them, they felt the red dust emitted from glands underneath the unholy fly fall on their heads. It was a burning, but an orgasmic burning. It was a wretched smell, but one they loved.

They walked away slowly back toward downtown, with red pulsing eyes.

Epilogue: Halloween

Wilson Greer had watched the entire events of the explosion from his pick-up truck parked just above John Ross Pier. When he saw what came flying out, he backed out of his space and flew through silent streets until he made the Interstate. Several times in the 3 hour drive back to his high hermitage he thought he saw red eyes in his rearview mirror, only to realize it was the backlights of vehicles that had passed him in the southbound lanes. By the time he reached Sweetwater, some of the gutwrench subsided and he turned on the radio. It was a staticky sermon of a local radio preacher denouncing the evil pagan practices behind Halloween celebrations. He flipped the station away and found a news report. The national guard was heading to Chattanooga. Something, some kind of terrorist activity, had occurred in Chattanooga. He knew better. He cut off the interstate at Sweetwater and headed east to the mountains.

*****

In a light snow shower he finally arrived at his shack on Old Smokestack mountain. As he stepped down from the stepboard, he felt his heart flurry and skip in his chest, and then, a piercing pain. He clutched his chest and tried to take deep breaths. He grabbed his flashlight from the truck and sighed with relief when the pain passed and his heart thumped normally, if a little on the brisk side. He flicked on the flashlight and headed toward his shack.

He stopped when he trained the light over to his chair underneath his shade tree. His heart went insane. Sitting in that chair was the tattooed man from his dreams, with eyes blood red. He was smiling. He put his hands together to mimic the shape of a church.

"Here's the church, and here's the steeple, open it up... and there's the people."

Here's the church, and here's the steeple, open it up... and there's the people.. Again and again. Spike seemed to move closer without moving his legs.

Wilson was frozen and could not move. Spike, now with enlarged luminous fly's eyes, finally came face to face. The flashlight scattered dampened light in the high grass. But the red eyes illuminated the scene:

In one quick move, Spike reached out with his left hand and grasped Wilson Greer's face and ripped it completely off. Then he

The Anchorite's Daughter

turned the flimsy mask around and showed it to the man with wide-open lidless eyes, a face oozing blood and fat and exposed new skin. Then Greer's eyes were red as well, blinded by blood and he sank into the night, saying his daughter's name for the last time.

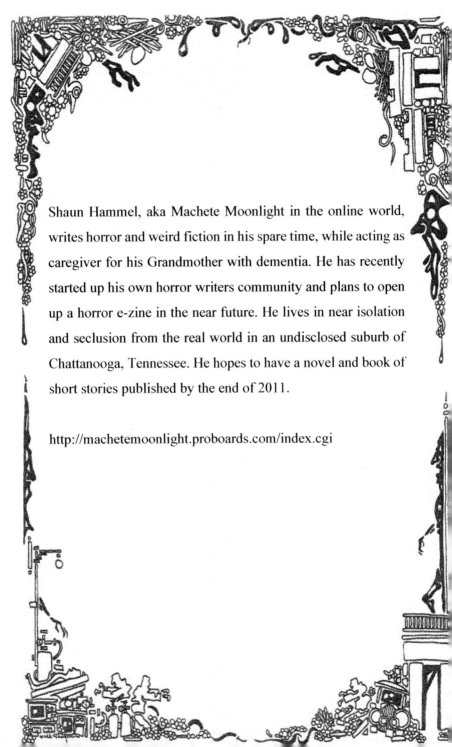

Shaun Hammel, aka Machete Moonlight in the online world, writes horror and weird fiction in his spare time, while acting as caregiver for his Grandmother with dementia. He has recently started up his own horror writers community and plans to open up a horror e-zine in the near future. He lives in near isolation and seclusion from the real world in an undisclosed suburb of Chattanooga, Tennessee. He hopes to have a novel and book of short stories published by the end of 2011.

http://machetemoonlight.proboards.com/index.cgi

Gehenna

Anthony Watson

Twilight casts pale illumination over a scene of desolation. Line upon line of tree stumps rise from the quagmire of mud that surrounds them, blasted trunks thrusting branches into the air to resemble the arms of corpses - blackened by corruption - reaching into the sky for a salvation which will never come. There is no dawn chorus to accompany the rising of the sun, birds have long since deserted this place of death and destruction. Those creatures which thrive now are the parasites and scavengers, the rats and flies that prey upon the dead, the lice that prey upon those waiting to die.

It has been a cold and wet Summer this year of 1917 which has turned the fields around Ypres – even under normal circumstances little more than a marsh – into a swamp, a literal killing ground in which men become trapped and drown as if the land is taking its own revenge on those who are desecrating it; as if death by bullet, shell or poison gas is not enough. Perhaps this place is cursed, twice already major battles have been fought here.

Gehenna

This is a true place of death.

This is Passchendaele.

As the first rays of watery sunlight cut through the grey twilight, a whistle blows, then another. More blasts follow in quick succession and then, like ants swarming from a nest, men flow from the lines of trenches, rifles held at hip-height, fixed bayonets reflecting the low sun's rays.

Through the mud they tramp, slipping, sliding, many have no option but to plough through brackish water which washes up to their thighs. No voices are heard, they march toward the enemy in silence, the only sounds the splashing, sucking, slurping noises of their footfalls in the thick mud.

And then the *thump-thump-thump* of automatic gunfire rings out. The pace of the advancing soldiers quickens – as much as conditions underfoot allow – as they march inexorably to oblivion. Bullets fizz through the air, many hit their target. Men fall to the ground, some gently as if simply lying down to sleep, others jerking violently as bullets tear through them, flinging them to the ground. The coppery stench of blood fills the air as still the men make their way forward.

The artillery begin their work then – high-pitched whistling grows ever closer, terminating in dull *crumps* as the shells hit the muddy ground and explode. Water and mud is thrown high into the sky, the ground shakes. Bodies are obliterated in split-seconds or are torn apart to fling bloody remnants across the battlefield as the shells find their targets. Limbs and body parts festoon the ground, lie in pools of water (red slowly mixing into the blackness), hang from the branches of the blasted trees. A Heironymus Bosch nightmare has become flesh.

Fear grips Billy Barnes as he stumbles through the mud. His breathing is ragged and, despite the coolness of this early hour, sweat pours from his brow. His heart hammers in his chest, the sound of it pounding in his ears but not so loud as to mask the fizzing of bullets, the explosions of the eighteen-pound shells, the screams of the men being mown down around him. His stomach cramps and he stops, bends over and vomits – acid bile floods out of his mouth to splatter on the muddy ground at his feet. He wipes his hand across his mouth as he straightens up and sees his sergeant standing glaring at him.

"Get your arse moving Barnes!" he shrieks, the words only just out of his mouth as the ground erupts behind him. Shrapnel rips through his body, shredding it, covering Billy with blood. He feels a tearing sensation in his stomach and – simultaneously – something hard hits his helmet. He falls, feels his feet slip away beneath him and then he's sliding, sliding, down into a shell-hole. He loses consciousness and a welcoming darkness engulfs him.

*****

He awakens to a world of quiet. Lying on his back in the mud he stares upwards, watches as pale tendrils of mist float past the rim of the shell-hole into which he has fallen. The sky has no colour but in its paleness he sees stars twinkling. The smell of cordite hangs heavy in the air. How long has he been down here? How long lying in the mud? Is the attack over? A vague memory comes to him, a blow to the head before his descent into darkness. But then a noise – a splashing, sucking – footfalls in mud but irregular, stumbling. Three splashes then a pause, three splashes then a pause...

Panic grips him – someone or something – is approaching. Friend or foe? He must move, lying here in the mud he is a sitting target. He rolls to one side to extricate himself from the black, clinging muck and screams as pain rips through his stomach. Through tear-blurred eyes he looks down and sees the gaping wound, sees purple coils of intestine spilling out. The sight causes him to scream again and - as he does - above him a horse stumbles past the rim of the crater, its flanks lathered in white sweat, the stump of its missing left foreleg jutting out from its body. Nostrils flared, its eyes are wide open in fear and incomprehension. Billy looks deep into those eyes, sees his own emotions mirrored within them. The horse is only moments from death and so, the realisation strikes him, is he.

"Yes Billy, you're going to die."

Billy flinches at the sound of the voice and pain flares once again in his wound. He feels something shift inside him, dares not look – afraid of what he might see. Instead, he turns his gaze to the source of the words he has just heard.

To his right, squatting on the side of the shell-hole, is a man. His head is cocked to one side, allowing him to look at the young soldier. A smile plays across his lips revealing rotting brown teeth. His gaze is intense and he stares at Billy with eyes that are black as night, black as the pinstripe suit that he incongruously wears. The white spats that cover his brown and white Derbys are stained with black mud.

"Who are you?" asks Billy, unsure whether this is a real person or some bizarre hallucination brought about by his injuries.

The figure remains crouched. Grins. "Ah Billy, you know who I am – the name's not important. Anyway, I have so many – too many to choose from! It's a beautiful morning and I feel inspired!" he glances up to the bleached sky, "let's say I'm the Morning Star – fallen to Earth!"

And then a flash of movement, the man becomes a blur and Billy's confused brain is filled with images and sensations that come and go so quickly he can not register them but which leave him with a feeling which is a mixture of intense sadness and dread.

Somehow, the man is now cradling Billy in his arms and the young soldier can now see those rotten, coated teeth, see also the dirty chipped fingernails, can smell the foul odour arising from his body. This Hell on Earth has its own obscene variation on the *Pieta.*

"How did you..." Billy begins but is stopped by the shushing of his companion (his saviour..?)

"No questions Billy, no questions." His voice is calm, soothing. "You're dying Billy," he continues, "not long left now. But don't worry, I'm here to help you take those final steps."

Gehenna

Billy's mind is in turmoil. Is this a dream – a nightmare – is he dead already..?

"No Billy. Not dead yet. But soon. You're in a very special place – let me show you."

They stand now – one supporting the other – on the rim of the shell-hole, gazing out at the battlefield. Pale light washes the landscape casting everything in a pale shade of grey, only the burnt stumps of trees stand out in stark black contrast. As he watches, Billy sees dark, shadowy figures moving across the acres of mud in front of him. They have no real substance and appear to glide over the ravaged ground.

"My avatars, my psychopomps" his companion tells him, anticipating the question.

Billy hears the words but has no comprehension of what they mean. A coldness has filled him, a numbness... "I've never seen them before" he manages to say.

The other man chuckles. "I told you that you were in a special place didn't I Billy? You're on the border my friend, the cold place between life and death. This is no longer the world you once dwelt in..."

"This is Passchendaele!" says Billy, "I'm Private Billy Barnes and this is... this is... Passion.." he slumps against the other man.

"This is my cathedral." He lets the young soldier slump to the ground to sprawl at his feet. He crouches over him, leans forward so that his face is only inches from Billy's. "Will you worship at my altar?"

116

Gehenna

A series of muffled *crumps* echo across the wasteland. He looks up and smiles as he sees the exploded shells release their deadly payload. Clouds of mustard gas billow out of the newly-made craters.

"Time to die Billy!" – the young soldier looks up at him, a mix of fear and incomprehension in his eyes. "Gas is going to get you Billy – even before all your guts fall out of that hole in your side!" He giggles, saliva drools out of his rotten mouth to land on Billy's face.

"Of course..." he whispers this, conspiratorially, "I can save you." He grins, cocks his head, raises his eyebrows. "Shall I save you Billy?"

Billy stares into those black eyes. He can feel nothing, not even the wound in his side through which his life is ebbing. "I'm Billy Barnes..." he repeats the mantra which has kept him from slipping into oblivion, "my name is Billy and I am eighteen years old..." he pauses, feels tears fill his eyes. Eighteen years old and about to die? The man with the black eyes said he could save him didn't he?

"Shall I save you?" shapes swirl in those dark eyes, distant, too distant to make out clearly.

"Yes" says Billy.

And, as the first tendrils of poison gas drift by them, the two embrace in a kiss. Billy sees the man's face loom towards him, feels the cold of lips upon his own and then slowly falls into darkness...

*****

117

They are walking, side by side, across the battlefield. Billy watches as ghost-like figures, little more than shadows, flit from body to body lying in the mud. They crouch over the corpses, bend their heads down to them as if feeding upon them.

"We feed upon the dead," his companion explains, "we harvest their souls. With every battle, every life thrown away we grow stronger. These are the places where evil thrives, these are our temples. Man's inhumanity to man provides our succour. This is where we grow strong..."

Billy pauses, glances down at the wound in his side – sees that it has gone. He feels no pain. "Will I grow stronger too?" He asks.

"Oh so very strong Billy! I foresee great things for you. Great things indeed! This world is ours for the taking!"

Billy breathes deeply of the poisoned air around him. There is no burning sensation in his lungs, no tingling of his skin as blisters erupt – instead a power courses through his body, innervating and energising.

He begins to smile, turns to face his dark companion. "Show me."

They do not walk but somehow they move across the landscape. As they travel, so their surroundings change around them. The mud and blasted stumps fade and are replaced by roads running between red-brick buildings and lined with tall poplar trees. In the distance, at the road's end, behind tall fences topped with barbed wire stands a brick chimney, black smoke belching from it to scatter ashes into the air. Even as they watch, the landscape changes again, trees replace the buildings, the road becomes a dirt track on which men, women and children lie dead. All are dressed in black, many are missing limbs or heads, all are beginning to bloat in the stultifying heat – flames leap from a straw hut burning in the distance. Another change, the temperature falls, snow now covers the ground. They see a soldier, blue helmet atop his head, turn as if to face them but in reality his movement is to fall to his knees and vomit onto the white ground. They travel past him, gaze down at the excavated earth behind him, see the bodies piled up in that gaping hole, see the flesh emulsifying, fluids running into each other and then the world around them changes again, this time the mutilated bodies presented to them have black skin, their blood stains dusty ground...

"Enough..?" His companion stands in front of him, black flies buzzing around his head.

Billy smiles, places a hand on the other man's shoulder. "No," he says, "there can never be enough."

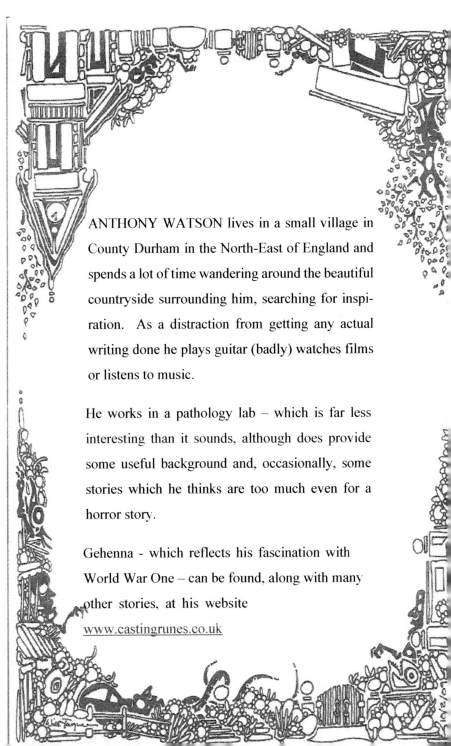

ANTHONY WATSON lives in a small village in County Durham in the North-East of England and spends a lot of time wandering around the beautiful countryside surrounding him, searching for inspiration. As a distraction from getting any actual writing done he plays guitar (badly) watches films or listens to music.

He works in a pathology lab – which is far less interesting than it sounds, although does provide some useful background and, occasionally, some stories which he thinks are too much even for a horror story.

Gehenna - which reflects his fascination with World War One – can be found, along with many other stories, at his website

www.castingrunes.co.uk

Last Laugh

Colin Hersh

I've always enjoyed looking at the world through a window, but that's only when there's something to see. A willow tree – giving me nothing no more to look at than leaves – blocks my view in the mornings. It's not the tree I want to look at though. I long to look out through the window next to it that gives a view of the whole front yard where my grandchildren play. I would give almost anything to watch them living in their prime, but the lazy boy recliner that I spent so many good years relaxing in, is in the way now. Why would anyone want a chair right there? Lilly's new furniture arrangement makes no sense to me, but she has always been her mother's daughter more than mine. Richard doesn't like it either and that's the second thing we agree on, loving Lilly being the first. The furniture disagreement I have with my daughter is second to the dis- agreements we have had about Richard being her choice of a husband. Even their children, my grandchildren, turned out to be rude and self centered, though I still love them.

As always, Lilly took me from the window to the breakfast table to feed me my plain oatmeal and tell me all of her woes as she spoons it into my mouth. I'd like to tell her that one of my many woes is that she doesn't add sugar, cinnamon, or any damn thing to the bland Quaker Oats to give me a little variety, but that would take too much work and creativity on her part, so I just sit and take it. This morning she told me that she didn't know what she was going to do about Richard. Richard, she says, has been going out more and more to the casino, spending more and more of her money. Her money? That's a laugh! I'd like to explain to her that it's my money but all communication has been cut off, as we used to say. I always just sit and listen. After feeding me she did a half ass job of wiping off my face before she left to clean herself, leaving me sitting in my wheelchair at the table alone.

Jenny came into the house and was obviously excited as she was talking to her friend, whom I had never seen before, about the things they would see in the woods today. Jenny's friend stopped the conversation when she saw me and asked Jenny who I was. I got excited, thinking I may get an introduction, but no such luck. Jenny simply moaned that I was her grandfather and she should stay back because I smelled like pee. Man that hurt! I know I smell like pee, but how could she treat her own grandfather so disrespectfully? I heard her friend ask what was wrong with me, so Jenny told her about my stroke. What was shocking to me was that she made it out like it was all my fault, like I had chosen the stroke. She told her friend about how she was forced to move into my house and live with me. She of course left out the part where she and her family was 'forced' to take all my money, throw out my belongings, and treat me like a old piece of ugly, smelly furniture. I was glad to see the look of shock on her friend's face at how she was talking in front of me, but she was quickly assured that I didn't even know they were there.

That I was a vegetable. Ever since my stroke, I have come to realize that hurt feelings can and do cause very real pain.

My family, pretending to be doctors, are sure there is nothing going on in my head because I can't move. Apparently the parts of the brain that control movement and speech also control thoughts and feelings. I can't talk. I can't even show facial expressions. My God, I wish I could find a way to let them know that my mind is totally undamaged and I can hear everything they say to me. I can hear every rotten word that come out of their mouths. Most of all I want to let them know that the boredom of sitting and staring is enough to drive me mad! When they see tears running down my cheeks they chalk it up to dry eyes and wipe them away with that smug and disgusted look in their face. Can't they at least sit me in front of the television? The money I had saved from a lot of hard work and sacrifice through my life are paying the bills after all. That's the ONLY reason they didn't stick me in a nursing home. They needed my house to live in for free and nothing more. If Lilly had to feed and diaper me to do so, then so be it.

Lilly finally returned and pushed me over to the back window. It was a pleasant change from the front as it gave me a good view of the river I had spent so many beautiful days fishing in. She almost never put me there because she didn't want me and my chair blocking their view. She told me then that she was taking the kids to the mountains for the day and would be back tonight. Richard would be along shortly to give me lunch and everything I needed in a few hours, so I shouldn't worry. With that, she and the kids were off. I don't think it was even twenty minutes later when the sun worked its way from behind the Moakley's house and glared into my face. I had to close my eyes to block the glare. It wasn't so bad, so I figured I could nap until my son in law got home.

Sleep wouldn't come, however. Instead, I sat and reflected upon my life. I had been a hard worker and much of my adult life's memories were of the factory. It wasn't great work but it was work. The smells of the hot sheet metal. The sounds of drilling and riveting. The heat from the line. I miss them. It was the familiarity of them much more than those things themselves that made me miss them.

When I opened my eyes, I saw that the sun had moved no more than had my arms and legs. It was starting to heat up my face now, and hurt my eyes. I hoped Richard would be home soon to move me. That's when I realized that the southern exposure of this window meant the sun would be shining through it all day and I was worried about my eyes, but I figured I could last another hour or so until he came home.

I looked back through my life some more. It was all I really had to do these days after all. I thought back to when I was a soldier in the forgotten war. If not for the television show MASH, I doubt America would remember that we even had a war in Korea. To those who weren't there it had lacked the passion of World War Two, and the self righteous hippie bullshit of Vietnam. Me and any one else who was there can tell you however, that it was a very real war all the same. We fought together, we fought well, and our cause was just. I saw a lot of good men die at the hands of the North and the Chinese. I was a boy when I went there. Hell, we were all kids when we got there. Men, if and when we left.

My face was no longer warming. It was now officially hot. The sun had momentarily gone behind a cloud giving me a view of the river with all the boats on it, but I was seeing spots. I realized bitterly that I really could go blind sitting here, and that thought scared the hell out of me. Being left with nothing but my hearing was a terrifying thought. Even with my eyes closed, my retinas were still getting a beating from the sun. I closed them again and waited.

In the war, I had been given medals. They called me a hero. I had taken a bullet in the arm and it didn't slow me down. They shot me again in my thigh, and I kept on going; I was like a juggernaut. That last one, the bullet in my thigh, still hurt today.

I was tough as nails when I was a young man, now I can't even wipe my own ass. Life is like that I suppose. I've heard so many people say that life isn't fair, but that's a load of crap. Life isn't unfair, it's just life. It is what it is. I think that philosophy is what has kept me sane all these years. If I let myself believe that I had somehow been cheated, I would go mad. Instead, I try to take things in stride and count my blessings. The hardest part, aside from the muted immobility and pain, is the humiliation of the diaper changes and catheters, but mostly the insults that my family believes to go unheard. I can even stomach the changes my daughter makes to the house. MY house!

Hours had passed with me sitting there in the sun and my eyes, face, and exposed forearms just plain hurt. I could feel my wrinkled and sagging skin growing tight and burning from the heat, and my eyes had begun to water with the constant discomfort. My heart skipped a beat when the phone rang. The sound seemed almost defining as it broke the silence. It rang seven times when the machine finally answered. I heard my quick greeting in my daughters voice announcing that she, Richard, and the kids couldn't come to the phone (with no mention of my continued residence in my own home), followed by a beep. Then Richard's arrogant voice came on.

"Hey Lill, It uhh, looks like I'm gonna be tied up with work all day so, um, I wont be able to swing by to deal with your dad's shit. Heh, no pun intended. Anyway it looks like it'll be all day and late tonight. Talk to you later, babe."

It's funny how his voice sounded almost slurred and I could hear faint music and what sounded like pool balls clacking together in the background. It's even funnier how Lilly never seems to hear these things. Not funny 'ha ha' mind you, just funny. A few minutes after he hung up, it dawned on me that no one would be home for a long time to get me away from the window. No one would be here to get me water, or even drain my bagful of piss and shit for me. I knew I was in real trouble. I no longer found the phone call funny at all.

With my eyes squeezed shut, I tried to play my game. My 'game' was my time passer and the only real joy I had left. To play it, I would think of all the songs I had ever loved and sang them in my head. I started with Joe Young's 'A Hundred Years from Today', and moved on to Ralph Blain's 'Going on a Hay Ride'. I was trying to think of a song to do next but my eyes, face, and arms started to burn too much to even think. The thirst was also getting very bad. Just because I couldn't talk didn't mean I couldn't feel the dryness of my mouth. I was even beginning to feel the backup in my catheter indicating that my bag was almost full. I knew that soon I was going to feel an agonizing pain all the way from my urethra to my kidneys. I wished she would have just left me in my diapers rather than repeatedly forgetting to check the bag.

Letting my mind drift was the only thing I had to distract me from the pain. I was thinking back to the summers I loved so much as a kid. Those were the golden years. Back then in the salad days we were the kings of our world. With school being out for the summer we were free to spend our days down by the river fishing, swimming, and even chasing some tail. The late forties were the finest days to be young and alive. One of my favorite memories was in forty eight when my buddy Jake and I went camping up in the hills with our girlfriends. We hiked around, drifted down the lazy river in our inner tubes, and just goofed around all day. It seemed that the day lasted forever, not just because we were having such a good time, but because the day really did go on for so long. It was the solstice. Remembering back to that brought goose bumps on my burning flesh intensifying the pain. Today was the solstice! Lilly had mentioned that to the kids when she told them she was going to take them out for the day. Slow but pure panic set in as I realized that I would continue burning behind this window for hours yet. No one was coming to move me or care for me until late tonight, long after sunset. I knew at that moment that I was in very real danger.

Some hours later I risked opening my eyes again to see if any clouds were blowing in to block the sun, which could give me some small break from the now excruciating pain I was feeling. There were no clouds, but there were two people cutting through our yard to go fishing down at the pier some hundred yards away. My breath caught for a moment when the smaller of the two, the son I suppose, looked towards me and pointed. The larger, the father I assumed, looked my way and waved. I wanted so badly to yell to them. I wanted to flail my arms in that unmistakable way that says 'I'm in trouble' to get them to help me. All I could do was sit and look – my specialty. I felt a tear, brought on by the blinding light as well as my panic, roll down my cheek as they passed by. Damn Lilly. Damn Richard. Damn them all to hell.

The pain from the pressure in my bladder caused by my of my overfilled catheter bag rivaled that of my face and arms. My eyes were almost completely shot. Any other time of year I might have been alright with only the bladder pain and thirst to deal with, but in the summer where we live the sun moves from horizon to horizon on the same side of the house. Between the glare from the sky and the reflection on the water my eyes were done. I knew that if I were lucky enough to make it through the day I would never see again. My face had a powerful and steady sting, as did my arms, but the fear lessoned. I was old and crippled, what did I have to live for? I couldn't say that I had no regrets, because when you get to be my age they were inevitable no matter what any one has to say about it. I regretted so many things I didn't do as well as so many of the things I had done. That was life and that's all I know. My only hope was that I'd die sooner than later, avoiding any more of the awful pain and humiliation that my life had become. I didn't want to die, you understand; it's just that I didn't exactly want to live any more. I sat resigned then, pondering all the beautiful things I'd never see again. No more paintings. No flowers blooming or tree leaves changing in the fall from a brilliant green to fiery reds and buttery yellows. Only the blackness of closed eyes and an empty heart.

By what must have been sunset my eyes were useless and my sunburn had gotten to the point where I couldn't feel anything at all on

Last Laugh

the outside. Third degree burns I supposed. My stomach, kidneys, bladder and head, oh my God my head, were at a level of pain that I had never before experienced. My tongue, dried and swollen, felt glued to the roof of my mouth and my chapped lips were fused together. I tried to open my eyes but there was no way for me to know whether or not I succeeded. There was nothing but blackness to see any more. I was alive, but I knew now that I'd have to spend the rest of my days having only my hearing and sense of smell for stimuli. All I could smell right now was reminiscent of roast pork and almonds. I'd give anything to trade my hearing for vision however, as I cannot stand to hear my grand kids tell Lilly that none of their friends would come over because they were scared of me. I can't stand to hear Lilly and Richard fight over putting me in a home or using my retirement money instead to pay for their cars and whatever the hell else they wanted to do with it. I acknowledged and accepted the fact that I now had nothing.

I don't know if I was unconscious or just too delirious to remember when Lilly and the kids finally got home. I remember nothing until late the next day. When I came around, I was in a hospital with an IV in my jugular vein. I only know this because that's what I heard the nurses talking about. They were discussing the irreversible damage from the burns. That topic led to how the complications from my sun poisoning, dehydration, and bladder and kidney infections would almost definitely kill me. I was in and out for a while and had no way of knowing how much time I was passing. This has gone on for what is almost certainly days now. The last time I woke up, I heard the unmistakable voice of Richard. I heard that sorry son of a bitch telling the nurse that it would be for the best if she pulled the plug on me. He explained how my daughter had been arrested for neglecting me and there was no way he could pay for my care and her lawyer. The son of a bitch! Richard went on to explain to the nurse that his inheritance would cover not only the care received, but cover the legal fees and fines as well as buying a little something for her, the nurse. She seemed to be listening intently not out of shock but out of greed instead as her continued silence inferred. Richard pressed on until that whore broke down and agreed to serve me my death.

Now she is telling me that it will all be alright. The pain is going to end. And she's right. The pain's gone and I feel like I'm floating. It's almost wonderful, except for the knowledge that this is it for me.

In my life I've been shot, in a car accident, almost drowned, had hyperthermia, and was even stabbed in a bar fight just after the war. I lived just fine through all those things. I never once thought I'd go out like this, a useless cripple being killed off in the name of greed by my own family. I would like to know what exactly she used on me to kill me, but I guess it really doesn't matter. As I drift off to my eternity, I can at least have the last laugh on the heartless greedy monsters I called family. My money, my house, my furniture, and my car are all going to the Veterans of Foreign Wars association. Richard and Lilly will have nothing left but my expenses and I can only hope their guilt.

COLIN HERSH has been a life long fan of all things horror. He is new as a writer but has hopes of publishing more shorts, and possibly a novel in the not to distant future. He lives and works with his wife and two sons in the United States.

The World Shall Know

Jason Whittle

Thomas Whiteman was shivering and shaking; sweat beads forming on his forehead before running down his face alongside the tears that were streaming from his frightened eyes. Eleanor Whiteman looked on, racked with concern for her seven year old son.

She was tall and slender, 31 years old but looking older due to the myriad of worry lines upon her face. Her figure would have been the envy of most women, but she was forced to cover it up with frumpy, shapeless clothes for fear of being labeled a harlot and jezebel, and being run out of town. No matter. She wasn't a lover any more, and she wasn't even a wife. Her life was all about being a mother, and right now her only child needed her more than ever.

She looked again and noticed the color in his skin fluctuating second by second. One moment a grayish ghostly pallor would take over his face, replaced by a red hot flush, that would then change back again. She was startled when she placed her hand on his forehead. He was burning up. She removed the thermometer from his mouth, and her worst fears were confirmed. In fact the result shook her to her very soul. For the mercury had produced a reading showing that little Tommy had a temperature of nearly 104 degrees. What's more, just a few months earlier, his father Joseph had been beheaded for the heinous crime of having a temperature just a shade over 103.

A wave of grief washed over her with the memory of Joe. He'd been a great man; bright, caring and respectful. In a time and place where women were subjugated, he had treated her as a true equal, allowing her to express herself and valuing her opinions. Girls had been banned from going to school, and consequently most women couldn't read, but he'd taken the time and made the effort to teach her. They'd kept it a secret, knowing it would anger the townspeople who would resent them for it. Not that Joseph had ever cared what other people thought. He'd always been something of a non-conformist, challenging the establishment and always seeking answers. No-one else in the town had ever dared to question the Scriptures, and he had gotten himself into trouble more than once for doing so. Once he even suggested that Governor Gerrard made them up himself just to make everybody do things his way. Poor Joe was fined two cows and got ten lashes for that quip.

The Scriptures told about the America of the past, which was a land of abundance and wealth, and had many millions of people who lived in splendor and luxury. But they were sinful and selfish, and never thanked God for their good fortune. They gave in to their carnal desires with reckless abandonment - out of wedlock, and sometimes even between two men. They consorted with the evil Jew and the talking ape, and the sodomite. The sodomite and the Jew were given all the riches, and they even made one of the apes their leader. This angered God so much that he inflicted a plague upon them so vengeful that whenever someone died he would rise again and kill the living, until there were hardly any people left at all.

Eleanor looked wistfully out of her dusty window at the decaying giant buildings in the cursed and forbidden city of Atlantis, and tried to imagine what life must have been like there before the plague. But even though she was probably the most intuitive and educated woman in the town, she couldn't picture it at all. It was only a few miles away, but it might as well have been on the moon (where Joseph had even claimed that people had once been!). So she went back to considering the Scriptures once again.

They went on to state how life should be lived now; that women should be chaste and quiet, and respectful to men. They should have children and look after the home, and cook for their husbands, and never want anything more. The men should work hard; breaking the horses, building the houses and farming the land. They should be vigilant in ridding the world of the Jew, and the talking ape, and the sodomite, who were inherently evil and had brought the plague upon the world. They also said that whenever someone dies, his next of kin, or a priest or doctor, should administer the decapitation ritual immediately after his death to allow his soul to ascend to Heaven and prevent his body from filling with evil and rising up.

The World Shall Know

In this little town, they had read the words of the Scriptures and taken them even further. They didn't wait for people to die any more. That was considered too risky. So if anybody got sick they would be closely monitored, and if they weren't better within three days then the decapitation ritual would be performed. And they wouldn't even wait three days if somebody's temperature rose too high. A thermometer reading of 103 or more meant instant decapitation. This was the fate that had befallen Joseph Whiteman, and now led in wait for his only son.

Eleanor applied a wet cloth to little Tommy's head, wondering how long it would be before Dr James got there. He would be on this way, that was for sure. Whenever anybody missed school or work, or were seen coughing or sneezing, then he would come around that very day. Not to offer treatment or cures - he wasn't *that* kind of doctor. He wanted to see if the decapitation ritual was required, and as proved by his diagnosis of Joseph, he wasn't afraid of saying it was.

Eleanor's father once told her that he could remember a time when the sick and vulnerable were cared for and looked after. When doctors existed only to treat patients, cure illnesses, and serve the community. But this was derided as the pointless rambling of a crazy old fool, and two days later they cut his head off. So nobody believed stuff like that any more, and Allen James was still the only doctor in this little town.

So Eleanor knew she had to get Tommy's temperature down before he got there. She gave him cold water to drink, covered him with damp cloths, and fanned him with the big mat. But when she checked his temperature again it had barely gone down at all, and she could hear heavy footsteps outside. Sure enough, a glimpse out of the window showed the portly figure of old Calamity James waddling up to the door, face red from the physical effort, but his big white handlebar mustache as resplendent as ever. A more repulsive creature she could not imagine, but she would have to hide her disgust for her son's sake. Right now, being a good mother meant being a harlot and a jezebel.

"Ah, the widow Whiteman!" boomed the doctor in a rich, deep tone. He was clearly somebody who loved the sound of his own voice, and also it seemed, loved reminding Eleanor of the marital status that he had bestowed upon her. "I hear your poor little boy Tommy might be a little under the weather today. Would you like me to have a look at him?" It was worded like a question but intoned more like a command.

Eleanor produced the warmest, most engaging smile she could muster and replied, "Oh, he's absolutely fine, Dr James. But, er.../might need a little examination." She ran her hands down her shabby blouse, tightening it in key areas and cupping her chest to outline her breasts. "I think I might need a *man's* touch!"

A greedy look came over the doctor's face that left her in no doubt that he would accept her offer. He was a married man, and adultery was a capitol offence, but the privileged position of doctor seemed to put him above such laws. And a lot of the children in the town had the misfortune to look like him.

Ten nauseating, ribcage-crushing, sweat-soaking, self-hating minutes later it was all over. He slid off her like a giant slug, bloated with self-contentment.

"Oh, thank you Dr James!" she began, trying to force herself to sound happy and grateful, whilst being respectful enough to use his title.

"I've been so lonely since... well, um..."

"Since I released your husband from his curse and set his spirit free?" prompted the doctor, before his face hardened and he sneered, "Spare me the bull, Eleanor. I'm not stupid. I know exactly what this was all about. But I liked what we did here, so I'm going to cut you a break and take the rest of the afternoon off. But I'll be back tomorrow morning, with Governor Gerrard and Sheriff Robertson. And we *will* be taking a good long look at your little boy."

And with that he was off, stomping out to his luxurious carriage where his driver patiently waited, as he had done outside most of the widow's houses in this town.

"Where you been, Mom? I'm scared!" whined Thomas, and his conveyance of loneliness and abandonment cut Eleanor deeper than the harshest reprimand.

"I'm so sorry," she wailed. "But I had to...*talk* to Dr James."

"Is he going to do the ritual on me?" whispered the frightened boy.

"No way, honey," asserted Eleanor. "I am *not* going to let that happen."

She looked at Tommy to see if he was reassured by this, but his eyes filled up with tears again. "But you let it happen to Daddy."

Now Eleanor was in floods of tears too; did Tommy know how hurtful his words were? No, he couldn't. He was only seven. And running a fever close to delirium. So she began filling an ice-cold tub for him. And thinking of what to do if she couldn't bring his temperature down. Because she had made her mind up now. Whatever happened, and whatever the consequences, she would not lose another member of her family to this damned ritual.

Eleanor got up after midnight to check on Tommy's temperature again. She held a candle near the clock to see that it was nearly a quarter of one. She didn't choose to wake up at such a time; in fact she hadn't slept at all. But now she thought about it, this was a good time to be up and about. Because by her reckoning, this was about the latest that they could start to get ready to run, and be clear of the town before sunrise.

Of course she hoped it wouldn't need to come to that, and a thermometer reading of 103 and a half showed enough improvement to tempt her into sitting tight, and hoping it would be okay by the time Dr James came around again. But what if it wasn't? And even if his temperature was down to 102 and seven eighths, he'd still only have 24 hours to fully recover before they invoked the three day rule. And deep down, she knew they would. So the decision was made, and there could be no turning back. They were going to run.

The next question was how. They had a good mare in old Bonnie: strong and reliable, but Eleanor wasn't sure they should use her. On a dead silent night her steps would echo and reverberate for miles, and such a sound would be sure to arouse suspicion. It might lead to someone giving chase. She had a good gallop on her, and could hold her own against any of the horses in the town, but no equine could outrun Governor Gerrard's horseless carriage. And then there was little Tommy to think about. He was quite a good rider already, but at the moment he was so ill that he'd be too weak to hold on. There was no way he could walk either, which left Eleanor to settle on the third option, albeit much to her own shame. The wheelbarrow.

As luck would have it, Joseph had bought a new one shortly before he fell ill. It was clean and new and ran smoothly and quietly. The old one was rusty and dirty, and had buckled wheels that scraped and squeaked in protest if you had the temerity to try and push it anywhere. It would have been noisier than the horse. But with the new one they could roll along undetected for ages, and with Bonnie grazing idly in the front paddock, no-one would suspect them of having gone anywhere.

She picked up Tommy as gently as she could, although it wasn't easy. He was getting to be a big boy now, and was deceptively heavy. But he was so knocked out by the illness that he didn't wake up, even when she lowered him into the wheelbarrow, which was thankfully bigger than the old one but still a tight squeeze. She was glad. Sleep was probably the best medicine available to him at the moment.

Then she had to fill up a sack with as much food and drink as she could carry on her back. She had hoped to put some of it in with Tommy, but the boy filled that barrow all on his own. Eleanor swore he was going to be as big and strong as a prize bull one day. She hoped. Then, after one last run through her mental checklist, and silent goodbyes to her old house and to those that wouldn't be coming with them, she took a deep breath and stepped out into the cold, clear night.

The first glint of the morning sun caught Thomas Whiteman in his sleeping eyes, snapping him into a mixture of consciousness and confusion. Where was he? What was happening? And why was his bed moving? Meanwhile, Eleanor was noticing that her son had woken up, and with grim irony she also noticed that he was looking much better.

The World Shall Know

She voiced this opinion, and was a met with a guarded response: "If I feel a bit better, do I have to go to school today?"

Eleanor pondered her answer for a long time. She also pondered why Tommy seemed to be so much better already. Was it the cool, fresh air? Or had whatever bug he'd caught simply ran its course? She then pondered whether she had made the biggest mistake of her life, and if she should turn the wheelbarrow around and trudge all the way back again. Finally she responded, "No, Tommy. You never need to go to school again. I'll be teaching you everything from now on."

Tommy smiled and declared, "Then yes, I do feel a *little* bit better."

"Me too," sighed his mother, but her weariness and physical fatigue prevented this from showing on her face.

Any sense of satisfaction she may have felt was swiftly banished when he innocently enquired, "Why am I in a wheelbarrow?". Then he made the connection, and asked accusingly "Where's Bonnie?"

Having explained the situation as gently as she could, Eleanor resumed her trek. It wasn't getting any easier. The handles of the heavy sack had formed deep, painful grooves in both shoulders. Her arms were seizing up from the effort of lifting Tommy and the wheelbarrow off the ground, and her hands were sore and blistered from gripping the handlebars so tightly for so long. Every muscle in her legs was aching beyond the usual limit of human endurance, but it got even worse further down. Her flimsy moccasins were woefully inadequate for any sort of walk outside, let alone a journey of this magnitude, and they had rubbed completely away in places to leave her bare feet exposed to the unforgiving terrain. Consequently, much of her skin had been worn away and her blood was soaking into what was left of her footwear. She would have collapsed right there and then had they not been so close to their destination. Because right in front of them stood one of the giant buildings of the cursed and forbidden city of Atlantis.

Eleanor felt strangely uneasy, recognizing that this was one of the pivotal moments of her entire life, and Tommy's too by association. The Scriptures said that this place was haunted by flesh-eating monsters who were once living people; soulless shells of men now filled with evil who would attack and kill all those who dared to enter the city. She didn't believe it and never had, but nor did she know of anyone who had actually been here before and lived to tell the tale. And that was the reason she had brought Tommy here; she knew it was the one place where nobody would be prepared to follow them.

So she edged them deeper and deeper into the heart of the city, eyes darting left and right all the time just in case the Scriptures were true. But they never saw any sign of evil spirits or the undead, and Eleanor put her feeling of being watched down to the years of paranoiac indoctrination she had been put through back at the squalid little town she had taken so long to leave. All she could see around her were signs of a better life; of a better time when people could eat fresh food from anywhere in the world, wear the most beautiful brightly colored fabrics, fill their homes with wonderful things and incredible fancy gadgets, and travel anywhere in their very own horseless carriages.

Now what she was curious about was why it all had to end, and she felt confident enough in her surroundings to really explore. All these new sights seemed to have chased the fatigue right out of her, and even Tommy had perked up enough to lift himself out of the wheelbarrow and volunteer to have a walk around. This may have had something to do with the massive toy shop just across the road, but Eleanor didn't mind at all. She was just happy to see him on his feet again.

Eleanor took him inside, and was as amazed and delighted as he was by what they found. There were all manner of outlandish replicas and figurines: flying machines, dragons and monsters, and horseless carriages that turned into metal men if you twisted them about in the right way. She thought that the children of yesteryear must have been very intelligent and imaginative to have known how to use all these things, and the adults very hard working and altruistic to take the time and effort to make them. But where did it all go wrong?

When they finally left, with the wheelbarrow full to the brim with toys that Tommy had carefully selected, she wanted to go some place where she could find the answers. And they found such a place a little further down the road – a house full of books. It was perfectly intact, if a little ragged and untidy inside. Some of the books were a little damp and smelled musty, and the pages would crumble up when you tried to turn them. But most were fine, so she sat herself on a worn out chair at a dirty table - which felt like the most luxurious suite after being on her feet for so long - got out enough sandwiches and fruit for a hearty lunch, and settled down for a long stay. Tommy wasn't going to get bored any time soon. He had all his new playthings, along with the discovery of a children's section where the books all had brightly colored pictures, and some of the pictures even jumped up out of the page. It was like magic.

Soon, Eleanor's head felt like it was spinning from all the new knowledge and information she was trying to take in. She was enthralled and enraged in equal measure as she found herself getting closer to the truth. There was no written account of how exactly the old civilization had fallen, but in piecing together what she had learned, she thought she had a pretty good idea. And there was one thing she was absolutely certain about: the Scriptures weren't true. Although she'd always suspected this, having it confirmed was still an overwhelming feeling. So she went outside for some fresh air, and Tommy followed her.

"You can stay in there, honey," she called to him over her shoulder. "Mommy's just thinking for a few minutes."

She took a few steps outside through the library doors before stopping suddenly in her tracks. Because there before her stood Governor Gerrard, alongside his famous horseless carriage (which she now knew was called a "car" for short). He was younger and slimmer than old Calamity James, with short, jet black hair and a pencil-thin mustache. Had he been of a slightly more pleasant countenance, he might have been described as "dashing", but there was something cold, almost serpentine about him that always unnerved her.

"Library aint no place for a woman, Eleanor," he sneered, before putting on a sickeningly false smile to greet Tommy, who had continued following his mother out of there.

"Hello, young man. Wow, you just keep getting bigger and bigger don't you? You'll be as big and strong as a prize bull one day!"

Eleanor was stunned by his use of the same simile, and momentarily wondered if they were really so different after all. But still she could read the malicious intent in his eyes, and it was making her very uncomfortable.

"Now you go back inside and play with your toys!" she snapped, one of the rare occasions she ever raised her voice to her son. Then, in a gentler voice, she told him, "Me and the Governor have got some talking to do."

"He's looking well," observed Governor Gerrard wryly.

"Yes," agreed Eleanor. "Very well considering Dr James would have cut his head off yesterday if I hadn't -"

"Yes, Allen told me about that," he cut in, chuckling. "And then he was ever so worried when you weren't home this morning. He came straight to me, and I came straight here. Call it a sixth sense if you will. Somehow I always knew you could read. Anyway, now that I'm here are you going to greet me the same way you did Dr James?"

Eleanor felt physically sick at the thought of it, and made no attempt to conceal her revulsion.

"Very well," spat the Governor, contemptuously. "It wouldn't have got you anywhere, anyway. So why don't you tell me what you've learned instead?"

"I learned that you got the name of this place wrong, that's for starters. It's called Atlan*ta*, not Atlan*tis*. And some great things happened here."

"I know all about that," said Gerrard, with a dismissive yawn. "I know all about the arenas here, where tens of thousands of people would come to watch displays of bravery, and falconry. And I know that Michael Jackson climbed Mount Olympics in only 19 seconds. Do you really think I've never been here before?"

Eleanor fixed him with a cold stare. "Then you also knew there was no plague here. You'd never have been brave enough to come here otherwise. Not even in that fancy "car" of yours."

The World Shall Know

Governor Gerrard said nothing, just gave a curt nod of the head and allowed her to reach her conclusion, "Which means you knew that there was never any need for the decapitation ritual. Which means that you..." she was shaking with rage, "You *murdered* my husband!"

The Governor held out his hands, palms facing her, in a mock apologetic pose. "*Murder* is a very strong word, Eleanor," he said calmly. "I was just following the Scriptures. Joseph was wrong, by the way. I didn't write them. But I do believe in them."

"What do you believe?" screamed Eleanor. "You *know* that the plague never happened!"

"It *did* happen," asserted Gerrard. "Just not here. And it would have happened here if we hadn't changed our ways. The Scriptures saved us all, Eleanor. Maybe not every single word of them is completely accurate. But what they stand for still rings true. They brought harmony to our town."

She scoffed with anger and disbelief. "We'll see how much harmony there is from the townsfolk when they find about this! I'm going to tell everybody. The whole town shall know. The whole *world* shall know!"

Governor Gerrard shook his head and gave her a sad little condescending smile. "I'm afraid you won't be telling anybody anything. You see, I didn't come here to bring you back. I came to make sure you *never* come back." And with that he drew his revolver, and slowly and deliberately lifted it up to chest height.

At which point Eleanor dived to her right, drawing her gun and firing it in one swift movement. The bullet hit the Governor in the center of his chest and he fell back, dropping his own weapon as a large dark stain began to spread across the front of his shirt. His eyes were wide, as if more from shock and bewilderment than fear and pain. Like being beaten by a mere woman was more incomprehensible than the realization of his own mortality.

"Joseph didn't just teach me to read," she explained. "He taught me to shoot as well. He said I'd need to one day, and I guess that's one thing he *did* get right."

Tommy had come back outside upon hearing the gunshot. He didn't seem at all frightened or confused. He just understood somehow, and without saying anything he walked over to hold his mother's hand in his own. Together they watched Governor Gerrard take his last breath, and then they watched his body for hours afterwards.

They did not perform the decapitation ritual, and although his body was already filled with evil, it did not rise up. And - Eleanor was absolutely certain - his soul did *not* ascend to Heaven.

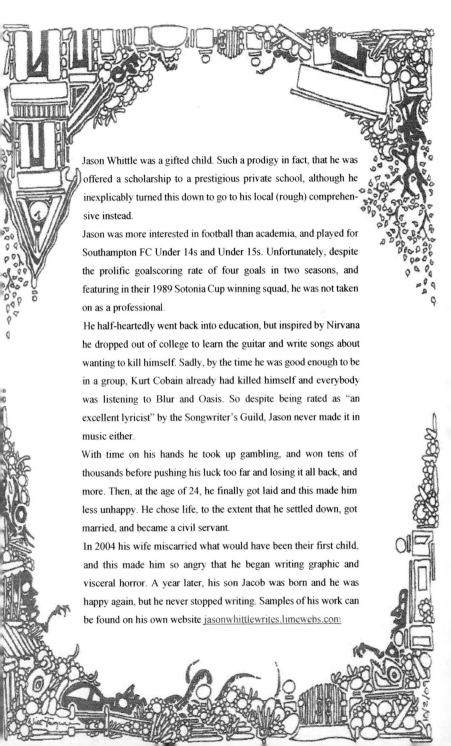

Jason Whittle was a gifted child. Such a prodigy in fact, that he was offered a scholarship to a prestigious private school, although he inexplicably turned this down to go to his local (rough) comprehensive instead.

Jason was more interested in football than academia, and played for Southampton FC Under 14s and Under 15s. Unfortunately, despite the prolific goalscoring rate of four goals in two seasons, and featuring in their 1989 Sotonia Cup winning squad, he was not taken on as a professional.

He half-heartedly went back into education, but inspired by Nirvana he dropped out of college to learn the guitar and write songs about wanting to kill himself. Sadly, by the time he was good enough to be in a group, Kurt Cobain already had killed himself and everybody was listening to Blur and Oasis. So despite being rated as "an excellent lyricist" by the Songwriter's Guild, Jason never made it in music either.

With time on his hands he took up gambling, and won tens of thousands before pushing his luck too far and losing it all back, and more. Then, at the age of 24, he finally got laid and this made him less unhappy. He chose life, to the extent that he settled down, got married, and became a civil servant.

In 2004 his wife miscarried what would have been their first child, and this made him so angry that he began writing graphic and visceral horror. A year later, his son Jacob was born and he was happy again, but he never stopped writing. Samples of his work can be found on his own website jasonwhittlewrites.limewebs.com

Blood Loss

Colin Drewery

Alex Poston walked with a swagger usually associated with movie stars. His body swaying from side to side and his head bouncing along in time with his shoulders. But this was no act. Alex knew his acquaintances saw his walk as a sign of arrogance and a willingness to prove himself. And unfortunately this was more often than not. Money needed to be borrowed, but as always the debt had to be collected.

At twenty eight, Alex had been collecting money for local gangster, Jimmy "The Nose" Malone for the last ten years. His small five foot six frame limited him to the more menial tasks within Jimmy's organisation, but his reputation belied his size. Non-payers were threatened with a visit from Alex and were always surprised when someone his size turned up. A few had even made the mistake of seeing him as a pushover and refused payment. These customers were dealt with quickly and violently and his reputation spread rapidly.

Now, as Alex sauntered down Brick Lane, past the old iron works towards the new housing estate, his mind went back to his first ever collection. A late payment, for the princely sum of seventy-five pounds, had brought him down this very street. The foundry was open then and Alex missed the smell of the old furnaces burning. Missed the thick smoke that hung in the air, which made it look like dusk whatever the time of day.

He remembered how good he felt that day. His first proper job for local business man Jimmy.

That day, almost ten years ago, was still as vivid now as it was then. No 13 Level Street. The address memorised. Some might say scarred onto his brain. No 13. How apt considering the events of that first job.

His trembling left hand lifting and dropping the knocker three times. His right hand deep in his pocket clutching an open craft knife. A muffled voice behind the chipped, red painted door and a sad face peering out from the opening.

"Hello?" The pensioner croaked.

"You got Jimmy's money?" replied Alex.

"I thought you weren't coming 'til tomorrow."

The job was simple. Get the money or cut 'em up, then come back for the money.

"No, today. You know the score. Every Wednesday, two o'clock, no exceptions." Alex already knew he didn't have the money.

"I haven't got it. Come back tomorrow and I'll have it then."

"Just give it me now Mr Preston or it will be double next week, and nobody wants that do they?" *Might as well give the old fucker a chance* thought Alex. But Alex saw the moment Mr Preston knew he had fucked up. Saw the moment his face dropped and realised this new

149

collector would be just as ruthless as the others. Jimmy would never send a 'pussy'.

"One last time. Have you got the money?"

"No." Alex had already guessed the answer and had made his move on the partially open door. He turned side on, dropped his shoulder and readied to barge his way in.

Both men tumbled to the floor in the hallway as Alex charged the door with his shoulder. The craft knife released with one swift movement.

The first slash opened up Mr Preston's cheek. The second sliced the bridge of his nose, exposing white and crimson beneath. The blade stopping short of a third strike with the tip poised just below the old man's eye.

"Now listen, and listen good. You got off lightly this time. It's double next week or I'll really fuck you up." Alex warned.

The old man groaned then nodded as Alex slowly withdrew the blade. Alex's first job done. Done with an almost satisfying conclusion.

Alex was no stranger to violence. Brought up as just another number in the system, he had spent his early life tossed between children's homes and detention centres. His casual approach to violence had always come as part and parcel of his society. Take it or leave it. But for Alex, mostly take it. Only now with this job there was money to be made. Good money. Not the pennies he could scrounge selling knocked off cigs and booze round the bars. But real paper money. Money that wouldn't earn him pitying looks.

Blood Loss

Now as he walked toward, perhaps his thousandth job, he walked with arrogance perhaps only the money could have given him. He reached inside the pocket of his green parker and tapped the butt of his Beretta. *Just to make sure* he thought. *Never leave home without it.*

More than once he had used the pistol as backup. More than once he'd fired it too. And now, as he walked once more down Brick Lane, he remained thankful he had switched his blade for something more substantial. His blade would never have stopped the four rival loan sharks who had tried to cut out his eye. The ones who should have brought a gun themselves. Instead, leaving him with only a deep scar stretching from the corner of his mouth to his ear.

Two of his attackers had died that night. Alex would never forget, but remorse? Not for this "cowboy." Collection and survival. Many times he would cite this mantra. Collection and survival. Basic, but apt. Basic, but imperative.

Alex stopped at the t-junction that headed the new estate and signified the end of the industrialised Brick Lane. Level Street, now called Grasmere Road, snaked off to his right. To his left Windermere Mews.

Alex unfurled a small note from his pocket and gazed over the writing. 7 Wainwright Close, Off Windermere Mews. Alex turned left and felt relieved when Wainwright Close was the first road he came to.The first pair of houses, joined at the garage, were boarded up. Two years old and never lived in. Squatted in maybe, but certainly never a legal dwelling.

Alex walked past, looking at the graffiti covered boards. "FUCK DA POLICE" screamed one bright red daubing. *Indeed.* Alex smiled to himself. His smile fading when he focused on the next artwork. A six foot high penis, complete with testicles, sprayed in black rising across the brickwork. It's creator's name tagged below the obscenity. "DAVE OV ANDSWORTH". "Fucking queer" Alex said aloud and continued past.

The next house wasn't boarded, but barely looked lived in. White washed, curtain less windows overlooked the unkempt front garden but the large black, painted seven was un-missable. A bin liner propped against the gate post spilled its rancid contents as Alex shoved it with his shoe, and walked up the path. The stench almost making him wretch as he continued toward the front door.

Reaching the front door, Alex turned sideways on and gripped the pocketed pistol firmly. He lifted his clenched fist ready to bang the door. Pausing as he saw it was open. *Fuck it, might as well take advantage,* he smiled to himself.

Pushing his way into the hallway he saw it ran for about three metres before ending at a closed door. Alex approached slowly and quietly, trying to subdue his audible deep breaths. Leaning close he heard muffled voices drifting from beyond. *This should surprise 'em,* he thought as he tapped the solid object in his pocket, and pushed the handle down swinging the door in inwards.

Jimmy Malone sat at a kitchen table, a shit eating grin beaming out toward Alex. The table bare, except for a small .45 calibre revolver and a half bottle of Jamesons. Across from Jimmy sat a heavyset second man. A man Alex didn't recognise, but knew couldn't be his client.

"Alex, come in dear boy. Take a seat." Jimmy motioned to an empty chair at the table.

"Jimmy? What the fuck?" Alex stammered. Then he pointed at the stranger. "And who the fuck is this?"

"That's just Sonny. He's a friend of mine. Now come, sit down." Sonny wore a navy blue suit and white tieless shirt. His black hair cut close to the scalp and a single diamond stud in his left ear. Alex watched as Sonny broke his gaze and reached for the whiskey.

"Steady on, that isn't cheap you know" laughed Jimmy. Sonny didn't share the joke and unscrewed the top, taking a large gulp from the bottle.

It was Alex who spoke next. "Jimmy, what the fuck is going on? I thought I was on a real job."

"You are. Sort of anyway. Now please sit, you're making the place look untidy."

Sonny looked up from the bottle and shifted sideways, making room at the table.

"Ok." Alex replied. "But put that thing away," he said, nodding at the table. Sonny scooped up the pistol and returned it to his inside pocket. Alex sat and placed both hands palm down on the table. *Just be ready, Alex. Don't you fucking trust 'em.*

"So Alex, I suppose we've got you a little confused?" Said Jimmy. "I bet there are a million and one questions going through your head right now? But don't worry I'm sure we will have all the answers you will need." Jimmy was still smiling.

"Jimmy, I don't know wha..."

"I told you I've got all the answers you'll need." Interrupted Jimmy. "We've got a problem that needs sorting before it gets out of hand."

153

"We?"

"Yes, us three. You see Alex, you are the problem, and me and Sonny here could be the solution."

Shit thought Alex. *I've fucked it this time. Jimmy doesn't come out of his castle for nobody. Patience Alex, patience. I could rush Sonny before he gets that pistol out and I reckon Jimmy is pretty slow.*

"Don't." Jimmy stared. Alex knew he knew. Could tell Jimmy wasn't messing. Jimmy had shot him a look like a parent scolding a child with the inevitability of punishment.

Alex double checked first to Sonny, who was again sipping at the Jamesons, then back to Jimmy.

"Jimmy, I don't know what the hell is going on but we could have sorted this elsewhere. Whatever it is, this is stupid. And why on earth did you have to bring this goon?"

Jimmy raised his hand toward Sonny, who was making to stand, and waved him back into his seat.

"You see Alex," began Jimmy. "you've been bringing me a lot of heat recently. Your techniques have become a little too violent and they haven't gone unnoticed. For god's sake Alex, two of my clients have even gone to the police. I fucking ask you, the police?"

"So what you sayin', Jimmy? You want me to reel my head in a bit?"

"Reel it in? I'll fucking take it off you prick." Jimmy slammed his fist hard onto the table and Sonny scrabbled for the whiskey. Alex fell silent. "I won't have a hood like you bringing me all this attention. You've done some good work for me, Alex but I can't have this. I'm afraid I'm going to have to let you go." Alex wasn't sure but he could have sworn that Jimmy winked just at that moment. *No, he definitely winked.*

Alex hadn't seen the figure enter the kitchen behind him, but he saw the polythene bag as it was yanked down over his head. His hands shot up to pull it free, but were met by stronger hands holding it in place.

Beretta. The word echoed in his head. He could have laughed to himself. *Didn't think I'd be carrying did you?* he thought, as he reached down trying to locate his pocket. *Got it.* His fingers curled around the butt of the pistol and he pulled it free.

A muffled crack filled his ears inside the plastic bag, and the Beretta slipped from his fingers onto the cold linoleum.

"You idiot." Jimmy shouted. Sonny stood over Alex, the small pistol steadied in his hand. "I said keep it quiet, everyone and their dog will have heard that."

"Sorry boss, but he went for his piece." Replied Sonny.

"Alright, alright, just pick it up and get that bag of his fucking head."

Sonny's shot was unintentionally cruel. A single bullet ruptured the abdomen, now causing blood to spill freely. Jimmy could see that Alex would slowly bleed to death, but there was no time to put this poor bastard out of his misery.

Alex slumped from the chair and joined his Beretta on the floor. The bag was pulled free and he saw his pistol also retrieved. Then he was alone. Blood pumping from the wound with only his hands to try and stem the flow. The searing pain kept him conscious for barely five minutes before the blood loss caused him to drift away.

The bright afternoon sun hurt his eyes as he stepped from the glass fronted building. An ambulance, sirens blaring, screeched to a halt somewhere to his left. A flurry of bodies surrounded it as doors swung open and a jumble of voices filled the air. Alex watched over the scene as a bloodied body was wheeled from the back of the ambulance. *Poor fucker,* he thought. *Maybe you'll be as lucky as me.* He was smiling now as he turned away from the hospital and headed toward the exit gate.

He felt strong. Strong for the first time in eight weeks, but Christ did his eyes hurt. He thought of all his time indoors, his eyes becoming accustomed to the fluorescent lighting of the hospital. And now, how natural sunlight seemed to be invading his eyes and burning his retinas.

Lucky is how he felt and lucky is what he was. He had lain unconscious on the cold linoleum floor for over an hour. His body spewing almost four pints of blood from the gunshot wound. A group of squatters nearby had reported the gunshot, but none of the services would rush to that part of town. By the time the ambulance had reached him he should have been dead, but against the odds he made it to hospital and was stabilised. Five blood transfusions and two operations later and Alex was making remarkable progress. Only two months after being admitted and he was out. Back on the street with the promise of revenge to saturate his thoughts.

Alex spent the next month cooped up in his flat avoiding every-one. The less people knew he was alive the better. It wouldn't take much for word to get back to Jimmy, and if that happened this time he would be dead. No mistakes, no leaving a man dying on the floor, this time Jimmy would make sure. But for now Jimmy was oblivious to the fact that Alex was still upright. As far as Jimmy was concerned Alex had died on the kitchen floor where he had left him. Maybe he was found, but Jimmy knew that Alex was known to the police and chances were they wouldn't investigate another gangland killing that deeply.

Alex had locked himself away and forged himself a prison. His eyes still hurt and he kept the curtains drawn constantly. He felt at ease in the dark and it made him feel as though he couldn't be seen. His vision would blur daily but Alex knew his recovery would take some time. It was the hollow feeling in his stomach, that returned each day no matter how much he ate, which gave him more concern. But this too would have to wait. He wanted Jimmy. Wanted him dead and everything else could be sorted later.

He still had some good contacts that he could trust and he had set them to work upon his release from hospital. He chose carefully. Picked only the ones he knew Jimmy had already fucked over. And each one had drip fed him information while he remained locked away. Nothing too solid at first as it seemed that Jimmy had gone to ground. But Alex knew he would surface sooner or later.

Almost a month of being locked away in the dark and fighting his increasing appetite, the breakthrough came. One of his closest friends had followed Jimmy to a pub where he had visited frequently over a period of two weeks. The source was positive that this was Jimmy's place. Alex took his word and the next day set out to fulfil his revenge.

Blood Loss

The pub was easy to find and Alex was sure he had collected payment from Jimmy there before. It all looked familiar but it didn't matter, Alex was here for one reason only. He watched and waited across the street before his source exited the pub. He nodded in Alex's direction before zipping his coat high around his neck and walking away down the street.

Alex checked both ways along the street before jogging over to the pub and pushing the double swing doors open. Inside thick smoke hung in the air and the stale smell of beer and sweat invaded Alex's nostrils. Several drinkers were seated and sipped dark coloured liquid that looked as flat as the atmosphere. Alex strolled to the bar his confidence, seemingly increasing with every step. A large, shaven headed man stood behind the bar his attention on drinkers at the other end of the bar. Alex picked up an empty glass and tapped it twice on the bar. The barman tutted then turned and walked down to Alex.

"Yes mate?" Enquired the barman.

"I need to see Jimmy. I was told I would find him here."

"You were told right, but he don't see nobody I don't know."

"Tell him it's Alex. I'm sure he'll remember me." Continued Alex.

The barman paused, studied Alex a moment longer then replied, "wait here I'll go tell him." He disappeared through the back of the bar and Alex waited.

Alex's vision blurred again but this time came an accompanying dizziness. It felt as though his brain was inflating and expanding to the insides of his skull. He grabbed hold of the bar, steadied himself and took two deep lungfuls of air. The dizziness subsided but his blurred vision remained.

Blood Loss

His stumble had attracted the gaze of two drinkers sitting in the far corner of the pub and both were now looking in Alex's direction. He felt as though the whole pub was watching as he straightened, mentally brushing himself off. He turned to face the couple in the corner whose faces resembled an out of focus camera shot. An orange orb glowed fiercely in front of them and Alex squinted, trying his best to refocus. The orb was about four inches across and appeared to intensify the more he squinted.

Then it moved. Moved slowly upwards and toward one of the drinkers faces. The floating orb then brightened further but was engulfed in a plume of smoke. The drinker stubbed out the cigarette and returned their gaze to Alex. *Jesus, what the fuck is happening to me* thought Alex as his vision began to clear. *I'm really starting to lose it.* He stooped against the bar and rubbed furiously at his eyes.

"Jimmy said you can go through." The barman had returned, and Alex looked up to see his focus had also returned. The barman motioned toward the open hatch at the end of the bar and Alex walked through.

"Hang on; I gotta pat you down first." Alex wasn't carrying this time, and the satisfied barman ushered him through to the back. The Beretta was near useless last time and Alex felt he could do better without it. *If I ever see him again I'll fucking rip him limb from limb* He had told himself. No need for weapons, Alex had never been as confident in his own ability. Couldn't place it but something was different. He was different and nothing would hold him back once he found his quarry.

Alex walked in front through a dimly lit, narrow corridor with several closed doors on either side. He was walking tall but his stomach ached. A gnawing emptiness that had barely left him since hospital. A hunger that he couldn't satisfy no matter how much he ate. No matter how many calories he consumed he remained famished and swore that he was even losing weight. But his diet would have to wait. He had more pressing matters now, and he realised his search might now be over as he was confronted by a large oak door ending the corridor.

Alex stopped and turned to face the barman.

"In there, just go right in."

Alex nodded and waited for the barman to walk back down the corridor before he opened the heavyset door and marched into the room beyond. Inside, Alex closed the door shut and took in the scene before him. Four large "suits", two left, two right, were facing Alex. Each one brandishing a large calibre pistol pointed directly toward him. Jimmy "The Nose" Malone sat behind a large mahogany desk topped with green leather. His high back chair forming a background for his head and shoulders, and almost overshadowing his true bulk.

"Well fuck me. Alex. Who'd have thought it?" Jimmy was smiling.

"Fuck you Jimmy" Alex stepped forward but stopped as Jimmy's "goons" began to look uneasy. "You left me to die. Did you really think I wouldn't come looking for you?"

"Alex, what was I gonna do? Business is business and I did what needed to be done."

"I did good work for you and you left me to bleed like a fucking pig. You should have made sure Jimmy 'cause I don't think these pricks will protect you this time." Alex's gaze darted in each of the men's direction, then back to Jimmy.

Blood Loss

"Alex, Alex. Try to calm yourself. What can you do, I've got you dead to rights."

Alex felt the hunger rise again. This time so intense he almost doubled over. But he still felt strong and his vision remained clear. Better than clear. Alex couldn't believe what he was seeing. Every figure in the room was now a glowing silhouette and appeared to be moving in slow motion. Their movements leaving heat trails in their wake. And what was that smell that was invading his nostrils and tugging at his empty stomach? Alex swallowed hard, saliva flooding his mouth as he tasted whatever was causing the smell.

"Alex?" Jimmy snapped his fingers. "Are you still with us?" But Alex was transfixed at what his eyes were showing him and didn't hear. Reds and oranges danced before his eyes and he simply watched as the "suits" slowly aimed their weapons. Aimed and readied. Ready for Jimmy to give the nod. Ready to put Alex down where he stood.

Jimmy nodded.

The air cracked like bonfire night as the room filled with bright flashes and plumes of cordite smoke. Tortured screams and shouts of despair rang out but were quickly muffled. Then silence fell on the room and an unnatural stillness hung heavy in the air.

Alex stood next to Jimmy peering down at his seated form. Jimmy looked up as the smoke dispersed, then stood as his gaze caught the scene before him. The four "suits" lay face up, eyes wide pointed at the ceiling and each deathly still. Their throats torn out and their blood splashed across the backroom walls like some garish paint.

"What have you done?" Jimmy never broke his gaze from the atrocity before him. "My god what are you?"

Blood Loss

Alex didn't answer. Couldn't answer. The hunger now consumed him to the exclusion of all else. The smell revealed to him. Blood. He could smell it all over this room and it was sending an erotic charge down the middle of his spine.

His jaw tightened and bulged as his teeth bit hard together. Readying himself to feed. Soon his hunger would be assuaged and his thirst quenched. Jimmy would be a good first meal. But Alex wasn't seeing Jimmy anymore. It didn't matter who was in front of him now, Alex could only see prey.

Jimmy turned and tried to back away but Alex had him. His hand closed around Jimmy's throat and he lifted him slamming him hard onto the desk. Winded, Jimmy stared straight back into Alex's dead eyes and spat into his face. "Fuck you, you....you cocksucker. Fuck you." Alex closed his mouth over Jimmy's throat and his tongue probed for the jugular.

Jimmy tried to shout one more time but only a blood filled gurgle escaped as Alex ripped at his throat and drank greedily on the exposed artery.

Alex walked from that room not totally sure of the events. His blood drenched clothes drew stares but no challenges as he walked from the bar. His belly full, but his mind in turmoil.

Out on the street the fading dusk was easy on his eyes but he didn't realise what the dark would hold for him now. Didn't know that the night would become his hunting ground.

A thousand questions raced through his mind but they would have to wait. Right now he needed to sleep. Maybe he would never find the answers or maybe he would never look. Even if he did, would he ever understand? Could he understand what an infected blood bag during his transfusion had turned him into? Many more would need blood. Many more would receive infected supplies. HIV could be detected but this "virus" was passing straight through uninterrupted. Alex had been chosen and he would come to realise this when the hunger returned and drove him back out into the night. Driven by an unquenchable bloodlust and a desire to feed. Compelled by hunger and the need to kill. But he would not be alone. Many more would succumb just as Alex had. Many more would need to feed or face extinction. But extinction would not be an option. They would feed. It was an instinct they wouldn't be able to deny.

And if the infection was discovered? Even then, it would be too late to stop this new breed of vampire.

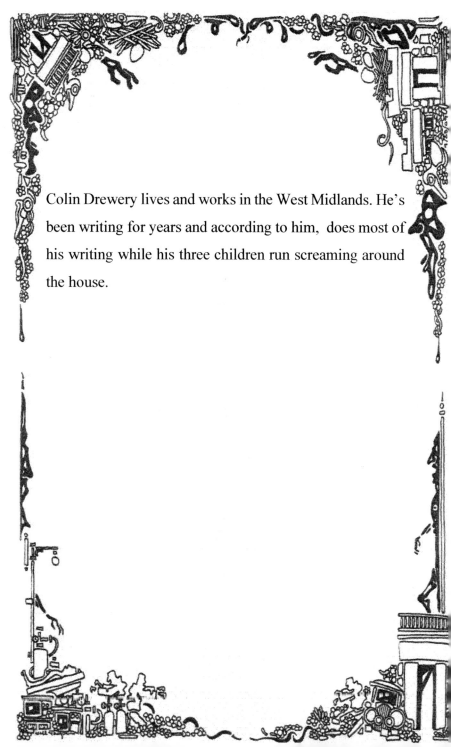

Colin Drewery lives and works in the West Midlands. He's been writing for years and according to him, does most of his writing while his three children run screaming around the house.

Vengeance of Hades

Joe Mynhardt

"Trust me," Nick said, "I can get us in."

The group of friends laid in wait, shrouded by the darkness of night and a few scattered bushes.

"What if they see us go in?" Sarah asked. "How do we know they're not in there already?"

Marcus shook his head. "If we stay here, they'll find us."

"Shut up. All of you." Nick glanced up and down the shadow infested street and then at the single story house in front of them. The house appeared pale grey in comparison to its surroundings. No lights shone through the large pane windows, and the front door hid itself among the shadows of the walls.

"I'm getting us into that house," Nick said. "Anyone wants to stay outside, that's their problem."

Nick hid his shaking hands from the group and, with a pistol tucked into his jeans, ran across the moonlit grass towards the door. He pulled a knife from his pocket and jammed it into the lock, fiddling it from side to side until it clicked open. He knew his troubled past would came in handy some day.

"Marcus," Nick said as the others joined him, "make sure you lock the door when we're all inside." Nick pulled Sarah closer and handed her the knife. Their eyes met for a brief moment of passion amidst the chaos and uncertainty. Nick took a deep breath, and led the way into the dark building.

*   *   *

The candlelight flickered before Sarah's eyes. "I'm so tired." She examined the others seated around the table – only eight remained. Losing two friends in one day wasn't something she ever thought possible. "Can't I go lie down?"

Standing by the kitchen window, Nick opened the curtain slightly with the barrel of his pistol, which was all he'd been doing for the last hour. "No. We have to stick together."

"We can't just sit around like this anymore, Nick." Sarah said. "We need a plan."

"Of course, we stay here, wait out the night, and leave in the morning. Together."

Marcus tapped his fingers on the table. "We're faster than those bastards out there. We can outrun them."

"No, it's too dark. They'll surround us."

Sarah looked at the others, yearning for their support. No one offered any. They were scared, and she could see it in their eyes. Tears rolled from her cheeks and dropped onto the knife in her hand. She turned it to the candle; the mirror finish of the blade reflected the candlelight like a crude prism. Sarah wondered if they would make it through the night. They just had to.

The thought of living without Nick made her grab onto the edge of the table.

*   *   *

Nick leaned forward, his face inches from the window. He rubbed his eyes and turned the gun away from his face to avoid an accidental death. A movement across the street detached the heavy veil of sleep covering his eyes. Reluctant to alert the others, he remained quiet.

He curled his finger around the trigger, and clicked the safety off. "If only the damn street lights still worked."

A crowd of people to his right advanced towards the house. They moved slowly but with deliberate intent, as if they knew what waited for them inside the house.

"They're coming!" Nick, his heart racing, pushed against the kitchen door with all his might. "Help me."

Marcus ran up to help while the others screamed in frenzy.

Nick heard the passage door slam shut behind him, yet he was too concerned with the heavy thumps nailing down on the kitchen door to look back.

A large crack formed down the middle of the door. A few more hits would shatter it.

The two men looked at each other and Marcus nodded. They'd been friends long enough to know what the other meant. To say *take care of Sarah* would've been pointless.

The two men stepped away from the door just before it ripped open with a loud crack. Nick aimed at the first figure beyond the gaping hole and fired.

A dark hand grabbed towards him through the gaping hole before it reached down to turn the knob. A muscular man with grubby blonde hair and pale eyes stepped into the kitchen. Between torn pieces of clothing his skin appeared to be festering in a discolored brown and black. A bullet hole was clearly visible on his chest.

"Run!" Nick shouted as he fired once more. Everyone pushed their way out of the kitchen and into the hallway. Nick stood at the hallway door and fired upon the army of intruders who forced their way through.

*   *   *

Sarah jumped to her feet after Nick shouted *they're coming*. She ran into the hallway and slammed the door behind her. She staggered through the darkness before a loud crash from the kitchen made her stumble and fall to the ground, the knife still gripped in her hand. The screams of her friends were deafened by a gunshot echoing from within the house. She hoped Nick was alright.
Sarah tried to push herself off the ground, but another shot sent her sprawling across the floor.

Vengeance of Hades

The passage door behind her flung open. In the dim light reflected from the kitchen she saw a small table placed against the wall. She held her breath and squeezed herself under it, her body shaking even in its contorted position. The light from the kitchen died.

The sound of people running up and down the passage surrounded her. They screamed in agony. Sarah covered her ears with both hands and, praying no one would see her, twisted her fingers to keep the knife from cutting herself. Flashes of light illuminated the passage as she heard more gunshots. Someone ran past her and slammed a door further down the hall.

Silence now crammed her ears.

Someone sobbed in the distance for a few seconds before one last scream filled the house. The smell of freshly spilled blood clung to Sarah's nostrils.

*   *   *

Nick, standing in hallway door, fired another shot at the attackers; anything to buy his friends more time. The creatures pushed the kitchen table aside, allowing the candle to fall and stifle.

He fired again. The flash of the gun shot revealed a hand stretching out of the darkness towards him. A cold, rotten grip seized him, its blunt teeth tearing into his neck. Blood streamed down Nick's chest as he screamed. He raised the gun towards the source of the pain and fired. A piece of flesh ripped from his neck as the force of the bullet pushed his tormentor away.

Vengeance of Hades

In the flash of light he saw more beasts invading the house. He pressed his hand onto his open wound and staggered down the hallway. Blood seeped through the cracks of his fingers. He almost bumped into a small table placed against the wall before finding an open door to his right.

Nick slammed the door shut behind him. "Sarah," he mumbled. His hand reached out into the blackness. "You in here?"

A dull feeling emanated from his neck and spread like a spider's web down his body. Nick dropped to his knees. He had failed to save his friends and his fiancé. Someone would soon come for him. The only question was, who? A dead stranger? Or a dead friend?

The screams outside the room became less frequent, until all noise came to a deathly halt.

*   *   *

The stench of rotten flesh floated through the dark hallway. Sarah knew she had to get out before they came looking for her.

She crawled from under the table and bit her lower lip, swallowing her tears. Thoughts of the unknown haunted her; where would she go, what would she do if they heard her?

With an outstretched hand she guided herself through the darkness. A warm liquid washed over her hand as she pressed it down on the floor. She gave a silent gasp and pieced her lips together. The blood seeped through her pants and onto her legs.

Sarah continued and felt the smooth surface of a door to her right. She turned her head towards the kitchen to determine if she was alone. A gnawing sound from further down the hall made her shiver. She reached for the handle, entered the room, and closed the door.

A burst of light and sound roared with a powerful blow to her left shoulder. The impact spun her around. Overwhelmed by a feeling similar to blistering coals burning through her shoulder, Sarah bumped against the door and lunged forward. She raised the knife above her head and stabbed at the dark figure appearing before her. The knife entered with ease as flesh tore and metal ground against bone. She let go of the knife and heard a heavy object collapse to the floor.

She turned on the light and stared at the bloody mess before her. Nick, the knife stuck in his chest and blood spurting from his neck, looked up at her with wide eyes. His skin was pale and his neck torn open.

She sat down beside him and stroked his hair. "You shot me,"

Nick closed his eyes for the last time. Sarah reached forward to pull out the knife, and stopped. She couldn't bring herself to touch it again. "Sorry, my love."

Sarah picked up the gun – only one bullet in the chamber – and pressed it against her head... then lowered it. Her hands shook as she aimed at Nick's head and waited for his undead body to rise.

Within seconds his pale skin lost the last of its remaining color and Nick opened his eyes.

The aim of the gun swayed between his right eye and the bridge of his nose. She had to shoot him. There was no other way. "I don't want to do this, Nick." Tears coursed down her cheeks. "Please don't try to kill me."

Nick opened his mouth and growled at her. The look in his eyes unveiled his hunger for her flesh. His limp body raised itself off the ground and Sarah backed up.

Vengeance of Hades

A loud bang turned her attention to the door. She charged forward in an attempt to keep the advancing zombies back. With her back to the door she looked at Nick. His head slumped to one side as he walked towards her, his one hand reaching out to her, the other dangling by his side. Her thumping heart froze for an instant as she longed for the grip of a weapon.

Her gaze dashed over the carpet till she saw the gun; if she could only reach it. Nick was closing in. His eyes twitched and his lips quivered. The wooden door banged against her back. Sarah brushed the gun closer with her foot and picked it up. She raised her arms at full length till the nozzle of the gun rested against Nick's forehead. Nick stopped, perhaps accepting his fate.

Somewhere within the horror surrounding them, their eyes met and all felt normal again. Sarah sighed, and lowered the gun. The two lovers stared at each other for a brief moment before Nick charged forward and bit into her shoulder with the ferocity of a wild animal.

The cold pain creeping through her skin and into her veins was nothing compared to the warmth Sarah felt in her heart. Her limp body slid down the door and she smiled – soon they would be together.

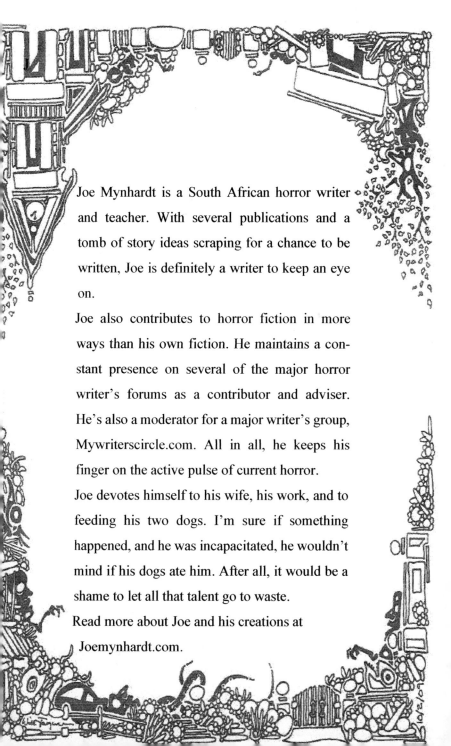

Joe Mynhardt is a South African horror writer and teacher. With several publications and a tomb of story ideas scraping for a chance to be written, Joe is definitely a writer to keep an eye on.

Joe also contributes to horror fiction in more ways than his own fiction. He maintains a constant presence on several of the major horror writer's forums as a contributor and adviser. He's also a moderator for a major writer's group, Mywriterscircle.com. All in all, he keeps his finger on the active pulse of current horror.

Joe devotes himself to his wife, his work, and to feeding his two dogs. I'm sure if something happened, and he was incapacitated, he wouldn't mind if his dogs ate him. After all, it would be a shame to let all that talent go to waste.

Read more about Joe and his creations at Joemynhardt.com.

Under a Setting Sun

Clayton Stealback

1 – Glistening structures of red flesh

Father Michael Stroud woke to find himself between sheets soaked in his own sweat. Morning sunlight struggled to penetrate through closed curtains, casting everything around him into a muted light and making his surroundings seem less tangible. There was a distinct smell of body odour in the air, too. Of course there was.

He slowly raised his hands in front of his face. They were shaking, and rightly so after the nightmare world he'd just jumped out of. There was something sinister about that dream, and to be subjected to it for the second night running only added to his sense of impending doom. Yet was it with any real wonder that he was dreaming of such things after the last few days? No, he didn't think so.

Suddenly, as if suffering from a wretched mutation of tunnel vision, the whole room stretched away from him and the images came: fast flowing, formless pictures flashing in front of his mind's eye. He closed his eyes down hard and counted to ten. By the time he got to three, the images had disappeared and the room returned back to how he'd always remembered it. He let out a long, shaky breath. It was time to face the day.

Throwing the soaking wet sheets off his clammy body, he sat up on the side of the bed and made a promise to himself. He promised that if he kept on having these lucid dreams then he would tell his old friend and mentor, Father Jones; perhaps he would know more about what they meant, although he truly hoped it wouldn't come to that. To merely put those dreams into words would be blasphemy in itself.

Here, on the edge of the bed, he cradled his head in his hands and reluctantly recalled the nightmare world he'd found himself in the last two nights running. In it, a blood red sun was setting, creating elongated shadows of the purest black imaginable. Anything finding its way into that black insanity would be swallowed up whole by the mouth of oblivion itself, he was sure of that. He was also sure that once inside that darkness, there would be no hope of escape. Yet, if by some vile, gut-wrenching design, you did make it out, you'd come back different, somehow. Tainted and corrupt. Ready to spew seeds of lunacy from the darkness of what was left of your soul. Yes, that had to be true. How could you come back any other way after being exposed to that kind of hell?

You couldn't. It was as simple as that.

Obelisk-like structures of glistening red flesh cast those shadows. Most were perhaps twice his height, but some stretched far into the fire-streaked sky. The ground in which they stood lay charred and blackened. Their ever-shifting sides lumpy and bulging, as if something living beneath the surface yearned to break free. This terrain, intermittently broken up by rivers of fast flowing blood, where winds sounding like the cries of a million banshees swept through, carrying with them the stench of ancient decay and imminent death, was surely the work of the devil.

That was pretty much all he could remember from the dreams, but he instinctively knew things about that world as well; so long as he was long gone by the time that sun set, he would be fine. A distant part of him mocked at how stupid this apparent insight was, but there was no part of him that was willing to test out that theory.

Michael stood, moved towards the window, and savagely pulled one of the curtains open. The world outside – his world – was still there as it had been all along, but it nevertheless gave him comfort to see it for himself. It was late; he could tell that much from the strength of the sunlight now flooding into the room. He looked at his hands again. They were still shaking, but not as much as before.

'That's your last exorcism, my friend,' he said to himself.

He'd said that on many occasions, of course, but this time he thought he meant it. The exorcism of Mary Jayne three nights ago had really taken it out of him. Sleep hadn't come at all that night when he'd finally got back home at four-fifteen in the morning. And when he'd found sleep two nights later, he'd dreamt about that hellish place with the glistening red structures and the setting sun. Yeah, that was it for him. Father Jones would just have to find a new partner. From now on, he would stick to baptisms and pardoning confessions.

Suddenly, a wave of nausea sent him running to the bathroom. He just about made it to the toilet before his stomach emptied, expelling thick yellow bile from his wide-open mouth.

2 – In the name of our Lord.

The last of his congregation ambled along the weed infested pathway towards the rather sinister looking iron gates marking the boundary of the churchyard as Father Simon Jones watched. He offered his usual sentiments while shaking the hands of each attendant, eagerly searching the row of faces for Susan Jayne. Why he was looking for her though, he didn't know. He knew she hadn't been sitting at her usual pew on the left of the aisle, two rows from the front. Maybe she'd decided to sit somewhere else today – more towards the back, perhaps. But no, as he shook hands with the last person, he realised that for the first time in what must be over five years, she hadn't been in attendance for the Sunday service. He hoped she was coping.

It had been one o' clock in the morning last Friday when he and his old friend, Father Michael Stroud, arrived on the doorstep of Susan Jayne's house. Make no mistake, Simon was a man of God and took his work very seriously, but he certainly wouldn't have gotten out of bed and dressed in his full robes at that time of night for anyone. He'd known Susan for a long time, though, and he'd been worried about the frantic phone call he'd received from her in the middle of the night. Mary (her daughter) had been sick for some time, and all the signs had pointed to demonic possession. Because of these things, he had agreed to go.

Of course, an exorcism is always best performed in pairs: twice the number of believers, twice the power. So this was where his old and trusted friend Michael came in. And that night, he remembered in absolute clarity:

'Where is she?' he asked.

'Up the stairs, first door on the left,' Susan said.

'May we come in and do the Lord's work?'

She nodded weakly, her appearance ragged, her face white.

Simon entered the house, closely followed by Michael. They wasted no time heading upstairs where harsh snarling sounds came from behind a closed door. It had sensed their arrival.

Simon nodded towards Michael then opened the door slowly, showing no outward sign of fear. An unholy howl pierced through to his very soul as he passed through the doorway. Once in the room, Michael closed the door behind them, and joined Simon at the foot of the bed.

Here they were, standing over Mary Jayne's twisting and writhing body. Her face contorting into hideous expressions of hatred and loathing as they looked on. Her arms had been tied at the wrists with white sheets to vertical bars along the headrest, but they were starting to slacken and come loose.

'Oh, look! The men in the turned back collars are here,' it said in a guttural voice, completely at odds with the tender face of the body it possessed. 'What do you think you're going to do, priests? I'll crush your feeble little minds with the power of my Great Lord!'

Never converse with a demon; that was one of the golden rules.

Simon leafed through his bible to psalm ninety-one, and began the ceremony.

'Whoever stays in the secret place of the Most High will remain under the shadow of the Almighty,' he read.

'Ah, story time!' the demon said and laughed.

'I will say to the Lord, You are my safe place and my castle...'

The demon continued to twist and writhe on the bed, flexing in ways totally unnatural to the human body. One of the sheets restraining Mary's arm broke free, causing Michael to run to the side of the bed as the arm flailed around wildly. With fast reactions, he managed to grab hold of it and pin it to the bed.

'Let go of me!' the demon screamed.

But Michael held the arm firm.

'Your eyes will see it and watch, while it destroys bad people,' Simon continued. He had almost finished the reading. It would soon be Michael's turn to command the abomination out of Mary Jayne's body.

'Whatever you do won't work on me!' it said. 'You're too weak!'

Simon finished and gave Michael a nod.

'In the name of Jesus Christ, I command that you tell us your name, demon!' Michael said to the foul creature which had stolen the body of this poor, innocent, young girl.

'I...am...Eluses!' it spat.

Michael looked at Simon. Simon nodded.

'Eluses, I command you in the name of Jesus Christ to be silent!' Michael continued.

The demon wailed then started speaking in tongues; an ancient, guttural language that made the hairs on the back of Simon's neck stand up whenever he heard it.

'I command you, Eluses, in the name of Jesus Christ, to leave this body now!'

An unearthly cry filled the room. The demon bucketed and

twisted on the bed, forming shapes that a contortionist would be hard pressed to achieve. Simon watched on as Michael positioned his hands over Mary's body and started to pray out loud. 'Thank you Lord for Your sanctification, I-'

In a quick jerking movement, the demon broke free and grabbed hold of Michael's arms. A split second later, it had pulled him down sharply to its face.

'Don't look at it!' Simon shouted, hurrying to the opposite side of the bed. 'Don't look at its eyes!' He grappled with Mary's arms, somehow managing to tear them off Michael and pin them to the bed.

'Finish it!' he shouted.

For one horrible moment he thought Michael would waver then, but he didn't. He took in a deep breath and continued.

'Thank you Lord for Your sanctification. I command any demons leave this body at once! I bless you Mary Jayne, in the name of Jesus Christ!'

The demon cried out again and bucketed up. Then the body of Mary Jayne was still. A moment of silence passed.

'Are you okay?' Simon asked, gathering his breath.

Michael nodded.

'Sure?'

'Yeah.'

Simon thought he looked a little shaken, but that was hardly surprising, was it?

'Okay. Our work here is done. Come, my friend. It's time we got back home.'

He pulled the door open then led the way out of the room and downstairs to where an anxious looking Susan stood in the hallway.

'Is it done?' she asked, a hand part-covering her mouth.

Simon nodded. 'She'll need a lot of rest,' he said. 'She may even sleep straight through the next two days, but you're not to worry if she does.'

'The...the demon? Is it gone?'

'Yes, it's gone.'

'Can I see her?'

'Of course, but be patient. She's not likely to be herself for a few days. Do you understand?'

Susan nodded but Simon knew that there was no way she could possibly understand. Not yet.

'Okay,' he said. 'We'll be on our way.'

'I don't know how to thank you,' she said.

Simon smiled and gathered her hands up in his. 'We are merely servants of the Lord,' he said. 'It is Him you need to thank, not us. I'll pop by in a couple of days to see how you're getting on, but if things change for the worse, don't hesitate to call.'

'Thank you. Both of you. I heard what was going on up there and it didn't sound pleasant.'

'All that is in the past. You need to concentrate on the future. You need to concentrate on Mary, and pray to the Lord.'

'Yes. Yes, of course.'

'Remember to call me should you notice any sign of deterioration.'

Simon walked along the hallway with Michael following behind. He opened the front door and they both stepped out into the night.

Susan (looking lost) lingered in the doorway.

'I'll be back in a couple of days,' Simon reassured.

Susan nodded, and closed the door behind them.

Father Simon Jones stood in the churchyard as the last of his congregation passed through the iron gates out into the world where so many shadows lurked, waiting to prey on the weak. He silently blessed them all...and he said a prayer for Susan and Mary. It had been two days since that night; he should go and see how she was fairing. And then there was Michael. He couldn't help feel a little worried about him, too. When that demon had pulled him down so their faces had almost touched, he hoped he hadn't looked into its eyes. He prayed that he hadn't, but when they'd been walking back to the car, he'd said something a little odd to him. He'd asked whether black for white had meant anything to him. It hadn't then, and it didn't now. Perhaps he should pay Michael a visit, too. He hadn't seen or heard from him for a couple of days, either.

'Black for white,' he whispered before turning his back on the tainted world and disappearing into the sacred confines of his church.

3 – Cold liver.

The phone rang again, but he didn't answer it. Michael sat in the living room watching a blank television screen with the curtains closed; the bright morning light had inflicted him with a pounding headache when they'd been open. Sudden nausea racked through him again, making him think he was going to have to make another dash for the toilet. As it turned out though, he managed to keep down what little was now left in his stomach.

Ten minutes ago, he'd had a couple of pieces of toast, but he still found himself excessively hungry, almost famished. Getting up from the sofa, he wandered into the kitchen and opened the fridge door. Inside were half a dozen eggs, a block of cheese, milk, sausages, peppers, all kinds of things, but what he was drawn to the most was the shimmering flesh of liver. It reminded him of the fleshy red structures from his dream.

'Bit too early to be cooking liver,' he said to himself.

He took two eggs from the shelf in the door, when a sudden sharp shock exploded deep inside his skull. The eggs smashed on the floor as he instinctively raised his hands to cradle the top of his head, as if he could block out what was causing him such unparalleled agony. Brilliant flashes of sharp agony inflicted his frontal lobes as images of Mary's contorted face appeared in front of him. He saw the eyes and those black circular apertures. There had been something frighteningly different about those pupils. Yes, they let the light in, of course they did. But they also allowed the darkness which had possessed Mary Jayne's body to come spewing out, too. And during this moment of unhindered enlightenment, he understood right there and then, that the darkness deep within Mary's eyes was the same darkness as in the shadows created by those glistening red structures of flesh. The same unquantifiable insanity lurked deep within both.

On that black night, when Eluses had pulled him down towards Mary's face, it had whispered something to him. It had whispered: 'Black for white.' And along with that knowledge transfer, he understood that a transfer of a different kind had taken place, too. A transfer not between mouth and ears, but between the eyes. Abruptly, the pain in his head ceased, along with the images.

After a brief pause, Michael returned to the fridge and pulled out the polystyrene tray containing the raw liver. He slammed it down on the worktop and savagely tore at the film cover until it resembled nothing more than useless, discarded tatters. Then he bent down (nose touching the slimy meat) and took in deep, ravenous breaths. Yes, the smell of raw flesh was invigorating, and before he even knew what he was doing, he grabbed the thickest chunk from the pack, brought it up to his mouth, and bit into it. With teeth sinking into the raw flesh, juice spilled down his chin where it collected in droplets and dripped onto the front of his shirt. Oh but it was divine! The taste! The texture!

The doorbell sounded.

Michael swallowed what he was eating and walked towards the door, using his sleeve to wipe away what had collected around his mouth and chin. He vaguely registered how the white cotton came away red.

'Parcel for-' the man at the door started. Michael saw the way his eyes widened when he looked up at him.

'Ah...parcel for Father Stroud?' he finished, still staring.

Michael took the parcel and signed the relevant papers then went back inside and closed the door behind him without uttering so much as another word. He threw the parcel on top of the sofa and ran up the stairs, taking them two at a time.

A ghastly apparition stared back at him from the mirror in his bathroom. No wonder the delivery man had looked at him with such an expression of vivid terror. In the mirror, he saw how his face had turned a horrible off-white colour, and how a big red smudge had formed around his mouth. There were splatters of what looked like blood down the front of his shirt as well. Michael considered his reflection and grasped hold of the cross which he always wore on a chain around his neck.

'Eluses, are you in there?' he said to himself, looking closely at the pupils of his eyes. If Eluses was inside him, that dark place was where it would be. Why not? It was similar to the darkness cast by those obelisk-like structures.

Yes! Of course! It all made sense now. The world he'd been dreaming about was Eluses' world and he'd been dreaming about that world because Eluses was now inside him.

Leaving the bathroom and running downstairs, three words kept repeating over and over in his mind: black for white. What that meant, he still didn't know. What he did know, however, was that when the sun in Eluses' world set, the demon would have complete control over his body. And the sun in that world *was* setting, wasn't it? Yes, it was. He'd seen it for himself.

Michael charged into the living room and picked up the phone. He should have known Simon's number by heart, but something was blocking it from him. He ran back upstairs to his office room. Here, on a desk littered with dusty books and random scatterings of papers, a black personal organiser rested on top of a haphazard stack of folders. He grabbed it and ran downstairs to the phone.

The dialling tone sounded in his head as he put the telephone up to his ear. He punched in four of the numbers...then stopped and put the receiver down on the table. Moments later, the voice of the telephone reached his ears, moaning that it hadn't been replaced properly. He replaced it under a dark shadow creeping over his soul.

4 – And now the sun sets.

Black for white. These words seemed increasingly important to Michael. In fact, these words and the memories of his haunted dreams were circling around in his head constantly. His understanding of that dream world was growing, too. There was life amongst the shadows there beyond his powers of conjecture. It was a chaotic, putrid life. Unprecedented in its malevolence and malice. Existing for the sole purpose of destroying everything good, transforming flourishing habitats into scarred landscapes of immeasurable torment.

Sitting alone in his armchair with evening light swiftly decaying around him, he watched the hands of the wall clock slip past six. And now, a feeling of unutterable evil he was powerless to stop, was slipping into his very soul, filling it with sickness.

Two large cases, bursting at the seams, lay on the floor by his feet. It would soon be time to leave this place...but not yet. He would rest up for a while, and wait for the cover of darkness. Then he would set out to do his task: black for white.

The phone by his side rang weirdly in his ears, sounding muted as if it had been smothered under a thick blanket. A small part of him (probably the part still clinging to the edge of the yawning abyss) horrifically understood that he was beginning to lose familiarity in everything around him. Everyday things were taking on a distinct alien feel, and for the last two hours, he'd been staring at the blank television screen with a vague conception that he had to do something in order to turn it on. Regardless of his strength of faith, these changes cast terror over his heart. Yet he may have been able to overcome this...this infection, had these been the only changes happening to him. But they weren't. Michael knew that he wasn't merely losing his knowledge of this world, but that it was being replaced, retuned.

He knew things now which he had no business knowing. For instance, he knew without any shadow of a doubt that the old woman, Molly, across the road, was going to die of a heart-attack at exactly nine-thirteen tonight. He knew someone had died in this very room, not far from where he was sitting. In fact, if he strained hard enough, he could see the body sprawled out on the floor by his feet. And he knew that a man (a dangerous man) shrouded in bright light was also coming, but this was of no consequence; he would be long gone before that man turned up on his doorstep.

He closed his eyes and allowed his infected soul to drift off into an infected land of the purest malformations of insanity. But the landscape of his hellish dream was different this time. Once, it had been a place of solitude and desolation. Now it was alive with malignant torment. The ground undulated like the surface of an ocean, causing the obelisk-like structures to thrash around. Inside those structures, stretching their skin taught almost to the point of transparency, were horrifically contorted faces, forever etched in expressions of agony. The shadows were deeper, too: a blackness not merely caused by the absence of light, but caused by something alive. He felt an almost undeniable pull towards them now, as if the darkness in his soul yearned to marry with the shadows and become one. Hot wind blew in his face, carrying with it the smell of rotting flesh. That smell was stronger than ever, as if an entire army of corpses were steadily closing in around him. Breathing in the foul air made him gag, and his stomach lurched as he fell to the undulating ground.

Here, balanced on his knees with his head raised up to the darkening sky, he screamed out as the sun disappeared below the line of the horizon.

5 – Nobody home.

There was no answer as Simon eagerly kept the phone pressed to his ear. Something was wrong, and hadn't he known that all along? Terrible thoughts of inconceivable happenings rampaged through his head like a tornado as he waited, hoping to hear the sound of his old friend's voice.

'Come on. Come on, Michael!'

Standing here, blighted by growing unease, he remembered how despondent Michael had been in the car on the way back home from Susan Jayne's house. Yet given the hour, he'd simply accredited that to tiredness. How careless of him to not understand the glaring signs.

'Come on, Michael!'

The phone continued to ring. This was the fourth time he'd tried to call in as many hours.

'Where are you?'

Simon shook his head solemnly and hung the phone up. He stared at the plainly painted wall in front of him, wondering just why he felt such a fierce spike of worry towards his friend. It wasn't as if they'd never performed an exorcism before.

With nausea coming and going in sweeping waves, he grabbed his coat, pulled on his shoes, and went outside to the car. A faint sense that he was forgetting something seeped into his conscious thought, but he couldn't grasp what that something was, and he wasn't going to hang around any longer until it came to him either. Time was short, he felt sure of that.

He hurried along the pathway to his car, got in, started the engine, and set off in the direction of Michael's house. The outside world was growing dark, making everything in it look ominous and sinister. Even the streetlamps with their orange-yellow glow looked to be poisoning the very air around them. Yes, something was wrong here. Very wrong.

*   *   *

Pulling up outside Michael's house, the cold hands of fear clutched at his heart. The windows of the house being dark was one thing, but seeing the door cast wide-open filled him with a fantastically intricate knot of unfailing dread. He knew instinctively that there was no point getting out of the car. Michael wasn't home.

Simon banged his fists against the steering wheel, all too aware of the fact that if he hadn't of spent so much time trying to get hold of Michael on the phone he may have got here in time. But in time for what? Revelation suddenly burst into his head like a brilliant light. 'The church!' he whispered.

With eyes wide and slightly glazed over, he threw the gear lever back into drive, performed a U-turn (carelessly striking the curbs on each side), then sped off down the road with a feeling of formidable terror sinking deep into his stomach.

'Hold on, Michael,' he said into the dark and empty confines of the car. 'Just hold on.'

The church, lit by those same ghastly orange-yellow lights, soon loomed up in his field of vision. He had time to wonder whether his hunch about Michael being here would be right as he made his approach, but if he wasn't, he truly didn't know where else to look.

The iron gates marking the boundary of the churchyard quickly appeared as he continued to speed towards them. When he could almost see the detail in the iron work, he pressed down hard on the brakes, screeching the car to halt and overshooting his intended parking space by a couple of feet. Unfastening the seatbelt, he twisted his head around to peer down the eerily lit path of the churchyard. A dark figure was struggling towards the door at the side of the church, wheeling what appeared to be two large cases behind him. Simon jammed on the handbrake, got out of the car without bothering to switch off the engine, and ran up to the gates.

'Michael!' he yelled.

Simon watched as the dark figure (now at the door) turned and offered a grotesque looking grin. It was Michael all right, and even from this distance, Simon thought the man looked mad.

'Michael, wait!' he shouted again, now sprinting towards the church. Such was his speed he almost tripped over his own feet twice. But he wasn't quick enough, reaching the door in time for it to slam shut in his face. The sound of the lock clicking into place tormented him further as he went for the now useless latch.

'Michael! What are you doing?' he shouted, banging his fists against the door.

'It's me, Simon! Let me in, Michael! Let me in and we can sort this out.'

There was no reply.

Simon put his ear to the door as if he might be able to hear what was going on inside, but it was hopeless; these doors were made with thick wood. He reached inside his coat pocket.

'Oh, no!' he moaned, his mind's eye showing him how the keys to the church sat peacefully on top of his sideboard. So those were what he'd forgotten.

'Michael! It's me, Simon! Let me in, will you?'

No reply.

'Come on, Michael. We can work this out together!'

It was no use and he knew it. The only thing he was doing here was burning time.

With a disgruntled growl, he raced back to his waiting car, heedless of the feeling of an on-coming stitch deep in his right side. When he reached the car, he took one last look at the church, whispered a silent prayer then threw himself into the driver's seat. Wasting no time with the seatbelt, he put the car into drive and slammed his foot down on the accelerator. The back wheels spun, leaving behind black tyre tracks and a thick smell of burning rubber. He sped home, smashing the speed limit all the way.

6 – Black for white, indeed.

When Simon returned to the church he wasn't able to park close to the gates. A group of perhaps two-dozen people had gathered there, and they were all staring up at the sky and pointing in frantic gestures. Simon followed the line of their fingers, soon finding the source of all the commotion. What he saw, hanging directly above the church like a vision from hell, made his heart flutter.

'Oh my God,' he whispered, slowly edging out of his car.

Recognising him at once, the people in the crowd charged up to him, fear plainly visible in their eyes and inherent in their actions.

'Father, what's happening?'

'Is this The End of Days, Father?'

'Bless our souls, Father! I beg you!'

Those were some of the things he heard, the rest of the voices merged into a drone of rambling noise as he continued to be awestruck by what had appeared in the sky.

Hanging above the church, a wild vortex had opened up, spinning colours of the most vivid purples and reds around its circumference. Yet this wasn't what was making him fear for all the children in the world. Inside the bands of rapidly gyrating colours, and seemingly expanding as he looked on, glimpses of a corrupt world containing what simply must be the purest form of chaos and insanity, was evident for all here to see. It was a world with undulating lands and tormented souls struggling to free themselves from great obelisk-like structures which, in turn, projected a darkness so black, he thought that anyone finding themselves caught within their shadows would surely go mad. To merely look at them was to sicken your very soul.

'Stand back everyone,' Simon shouted. 'Stand back, I say!'

They did, of course, forming a shambling aisle for him to walk down; people at the back jostling for positions at the front. All begging for forgiveness. All reaching out in a vast struggle just to lay their hands on him, as if touching him would somehow sanctify their existence.

'Go home!' he told them in no uncertain terms. 'There's nothing you can do here. So go home and pray!'

No one left; they all just stood around, first looking dumbfounded at each other, then looking back at him for reassurance. But he had no words for them. Besides, these people were not his priority. It tugged at his heart, but he turned his back on them and their cries for salvation, and crossed himself as he walked down the path towards the church.

At the side door, he slotted the key into the lock and turned it. After a small click, he pressed down on the latch and applied his weight against the wooden arched door.

It wouldn't open. Michael must have locked it from the inside, too.

Panic, made all the more intense by standing directly beneath the hellish world swirling above his head, very nearly took control of him. From here, he could smell the putrid essence of rotting flesh, could feel the lingering presence of death all around him. Nothing good could ever be refined from that world, he was sure.

Pressing his back up against the wall of the church to make himself as flat as he could, he considered the options. He could try the front doors, but if Michael had been shrewd enough to lock the door at the side, the chances are that he would have locked the front doors from the inside, too. There was, however, one other door around the back. This entrance led into a small office. Surely it had to be worth a try.

Hugging the wall, he made his way to the door at the back, knowing that if too much of him came away from the protection of the church, something would come out of the vortex to snatch him up and cast him out into that world of eternal pain and suffering. His progress was slow, but at least it was progress.

'Please, God, give me the strength I need,' he whispered upon reaching the door. Then he settled himself, breathing in deeply. He inserted the key into the lock and gave it a turn. There was a small click. Uttering a silent prayer, he pushed firmly against the door. It gave, swinging open on screeching hinges which sounded impossibly loud to his adrenalin fuelled senses. The room inside was dark, causing him to creep inside in the fear that the very ground might give way on him at any moment. But it didn't. At least, not yet.

On his left was a desk made untidy by the amount of open books and papers which had been scattered across its scarred wooden surface. It all looked so alien to him, so...unfamiliar. Yet it had only been earlier today when he'd sat at this very table, gathering material for the next Sunday service. It had never crossed his mind then, that there might not ever be another Sunday service.

Another wooden door, shutting off an arched passageway beyond, grew in his vision as he approached it. Of course, Michael could have locked this one from the inside instead, but when he pressed down on the latch and pulled the door towards him, he found that he hadn't. Still breathing in deeply, he walked through the doorway into a passage where distorted shadows of God knows what flickered along the walls, seeming to dance to the sounds of unutterable chanting coming from the grand opening ahead.

'God help me,' he whispered, slowly edging along.

It suddenly occurred to him that he might just have the upper hand here. This passageway would bring him out directly behind the altar, and if he was lucky, Michael would be facing the front. Perhaps he would be able to sneak up behind him and stop him from playing any further part in this...this abomination.

'Eluses, are you here?' he whispered.

Simon kept to the shadows as he gradually reached the end of the passageway, and as he had dared to hope, Michael (his body, at least) was at the altar, facing the front. For perhaps the first time today, a trace of a smile touched his face – it seemed even a demon had to have some etiquette when in attendance with the Lord.

Yet his smile was short-lived. 'Oh, my God!' he muttered.

The ceiling above the altar had turned transparent, giving a direct line of sight into that world of twisted insanity. The very air stunk of rotting flesh as it swam down to explore the contours of his face. It carried with it agonising cries, causing him to double up and clutch at his stomach.

With his new viewpoint close to the floor, he saw candles littered all around the altar and strewn down the aisles. Some lay whole, others lay shattered in pieces as if they'd been thrown to the ground with considerable force. There were hundreds of them; all discarded from their once elevated positions on silver holders. And now, candles of the purest black sat burning in their place. Black for white, indeed.

7 – They all need flesh!

One of the fleshy structures from the world above stretched down towards the church, seeming to merge into the ceiling. Simon knew time was growing short and without a moment's thought, he launched himself at Michael.

Within inches of reaching him, Michael twisted around with an unnatural speed. The expression on his face both grotesque and malevolent, filled Simon with such a composition of dismay and terror, it was a wonder his heart didn't stop right there and then. He saw Michael raise the palm of his hand up to him, then a feeling of someone shoving him violently back exploded in the centre of his chest. All the wind in his lungs shot out of him as his feet left the ground and his body flew backwards. He landed heavily on his back, savagely scattering shattered pieces of candles in all directions as he ploughed through them. The wall brought about an abrupt stop when the back of his head collided against it with a hollow thump. Dozens of flashing dots appeared in front of his eyes, and for a moment he thought he was about to lose consciousness.

'Well hello there, Father Jones,' Michael said. 'Welcome to my new sanctum of worship. Do you like what I've done to the place?'

'Michael, you have to stop this!' Simon slurred between rasping gasps of breath.

'Michael's not here any more!' it cackled. 'He's up there somewhere.' It pointed to the hellish world within the vortex that was (Simon realised) gyrating directly above the altar.

'Hark, I think I can hear him,' it continued. 'Yes, I truly believe I can. Can you, Father?'

Under a Setting Sun

Simon stumbled to his feet, whereby his vision darkened, and a wave of dizziness almost sent him sprawling back down onto the cold hard floor.

'Whoa there, Father! You've just had one hell of a fall. I wouldn't be going all crazy if I were you,' it said, shaking Michael's head. 'Look at the state of you. You really should take better care of yourself.'

Simon fought the sickness deep inside himself and stood tall, puffing out his chest in a mark of defiance.

'I command you, Eluses, in the name of Jesus Christ, to leave Michael's body. Now!'

'Ah, so you remember me. I'm touched.'

Simon paused. 'What do you want?' he asked.

Never converse with a demon, that was one of the rules. Simon was well aware of that, but he didn't think the tried and tested methods were going to work this time.

'What do I want?' the demon laughed. 'Oh, Father, I'm disappointed in you. You of all people should know the answer to that.'

'Humour me, demon!'

Eluses looked up at the vortex and sucked in a deep breath. 'Oh, just smell that air. Isn't it divine?' It cast Michael's eyes back down towards him and continued. 'For far too long, your kind have had free reign over this world. For far too long we have been cast out in the shadows, having to live in squalor like second-rate beings, rejects from what you call your world. That's all about to change, Father. Now is our time!' It paused and tilted Michael's head to one side. 'Do you hear him?'

Simon followed Eluses' wide-eyed gaze towards the large stained glass window on the west side of the church, and watched in a perverse mix of horror and fascination as the colours in the window bled away, leaving behind shadows of murky grey. Suddenly, the window started to buckle inward as an enormous face pressed up against the glass. It should have smashed the window into pieces, but it didn't. Instead, the window acted as some kind of super-elastic barrier, keeping whatever hell beyond that glass out. For now, at least.

'Here he comes!' Eluses screamed.

That face pressed up against the glass looked almost animal in its composition. To see it protruding deeper into the House of God filled Simon with unsurpassed dread. How could this be happening? Why was God allowing this to happen? His faith wavered.

'Yes,' Eluses said. 'Why not join us? You'll be the first of your kind to witness the coming of our Lord.'

'Never!' Simon spat.

The face in the widow twisted in his direction. Simon looked away sharply. To look into that face would be to look into the darkest depths imaginable, to taint your soul with misery and immeasurable torment, forever.

'Then die like the rest!' Eluses replied. 'It's time!'

Sublime terror encompassed him as he watched Eluses pull the world inside the vortex down towards them. Streams of dust fell from the ceiling as the whole place shook. Lines of pews shifted out of position and became askew. A huge crack appeared close to the ceiling in the front façade, creating a teeth-clenching grinding sound as it crept ever downward.

'Come to me, my friends. Our time is now,' Eluses shouted above the noise.

Under a Setting Sun

The ground suddenly opened up a few feet away from where Simon was now leaning against the wall. From out of the yawning hole, a fleshy structure rose up, disregarding anything which got in its way. He watched in utter revulsion (hearing Eluses laughing wildly) as twisted faces, all screaming out in agony, stretched the flesh of this hellish structure taught. And oh God, there were children's faces amongst them, too.

Then came the hands. Grasping hands, protruding from the elastic flesh. Reaching out, all trying to touch him. He thought this might well be their last chance of whatever would now pass as salvation for their damned souls, and he slowly reached out to meet them. But just before fingers touched, he was thrown back by the uprising of another fleshy structure.

'Oh just listen to them!' Eluses cried. 'At last they've found their voices. Don't they sound magnificent?'

Simon cowered back against the wall as the screams of the damned echoed around the inside of the church. The acoustics of the place magnifying and intensifying the sound, creating a chorus of unprecedented torment.

'Michael, stop this!' Simon shouted. 'I know you're in there somewhere, so stop this now!'

Eluses whipped around to face him. Michael's eyes were horribly bloodshot, and there was blood oozing out of his ears.

'Michael, it's me, Simon. Stop this! Search for the light, search for the Lord. You are in the House of God, Michael!'

Simon was all too aware of the face in the stained glass window staring at him. He could feel its gaze piercing through to his very soul, could feel the taint and the infection of indescribable evil trying to take hold. The temptation to look was almost unbearable, testing his will to its absolute limit.

'Help us, Michael! In the name of Jesus Christ, help us!'

'Michael is not here, Father!' Eluses spat, spewing blood from Michael's mouth along with a couple of projectiles Simon thought were teeth.

'Michael's body isn't strong enough for your purposes, Eluses. Can't you see that? You're destroying your host!'

'Oh, it's strong enough,' he replied, grinning. 'Although I fear that Michael will never get to experience the new world. A world of pure chaos. Pure evil. Such a shame after everything he's been through, don't you think?' Blood was now trickling from Michael's nose as well as from his mouth and ears.

The ground opened up again, inches from where Simon was standing, the force of it throwing him back as another structure from hell rose up within arms length. Faces and hands struggled to reach him, stretching its flesh taught almost to the point of transparency.

'Ah, they can sense you, Father. That's good,' Eluses said. 'Well? What are you waiting for? Do your job and bless those poor, wretched souls!'

Inconsolable repulsion filled his heart as he watched those groping hands.

'Lord, give me strength,' he uttered. Then, he reached out.

With that same lightning speed he'd seen Eluses possess, one of the hands clasped tightly around his. Then another. And another. He screamed as razor sharp fingernails dug into his skin, puncturing through to the bone. With the initial shock passing, he tore his hand back sharply, threads of shredded skin hanging limply off his hand.

'Yes! It's flesh they want, Father. We all want flesh!' Eluses screamed, blood flying from Michael's mouth like a faucet. 'And now,' he continued, 'it's time to end this. It's time to call upon my Great Lord and grant him access back into the world from which he was shunned. This is our time, Father. Behold the coming of the Dark Lord himself!'

Eluses raised his hands up into the air and the whole place shook with the force of more fleshy structures sprouting up from everywhere. One rose up directly behind Eluses, and Simon knew that this was the moment he'd been hoping for. It was now or never.

Suddenly and without warning, he got to his feet and charged at Eluses. The demon was quick, but inside Michael's rapidly deteriorating body, it didn't have time to react before he slammed into it (causing a mixture of blood, bile, and teeth to come spraying out of Michael's mouth) and shoved it up against the fleshy structure.

'If it's flesh they want, then flesh they shall have!' Simon screamed.

'No!' Eluses yelled.

As soon as Michael's body came into contact with the structure, dozens of hands thrust out of it quick as lightning, pinning Eluses to its foul surface. Simon turned his back on the grisly scene; if Eluses could jump into Michael's body...

'Simon! Simon, help me!' Michael screamed.

Simon's heart sunk. Tears brimmed in his eyes as he listened to chunks of flesh being torn from his friend's body.

'Simon, it's me, Michael! Help me!'

Under a Setting Sun

Even though he closed his eyes down hard and pressed his hands over his ears, it wasn't enough to prevent Michael's screams of agony and sounds of ripping flesh from reaching his ears. It wasn't enough to stop his imagination showing him what was happening. His friend was dying only a few feet away, and he'd turned his back on him.

'Simon! Please!'

'I can't help you!' he shouted. 'I'm sorry, Michael, but I can't help you!'

He collapsed to his knees, surrounded by sounds of tearing flesh and agonising screams. There was a sickening crack then Michael spoke no more.

Moments later, the fleshy structures started to sink back into the ground. Then, a cry of immense anguish reached his ears, followed by the sound of shattering glass from what must have been all of the windows in the place disintegrating. He remained curled up on the floor, cradling his head in his arms: something was behind him; he felt its terrible presence. All that was evil and corrupt and black lingered around him. It was perhaps the very essence of hell itself, a fragment of unspoken madness and chaos. Yet the urge to look and see was insanely alluring, all consuming.

Yes, the temptation was crushing. He didn't know how much more he could stand, but just as his resolve was weakening, the dark lingering presence vanished. Eluses was finally gone. It was over.

Slowly and shakily, Simon rose to his feet. The church was close to a ruin: the windows were all smashed; great cracks from the ceiling stretched all the way to the ground; the floor (littered with shattered candles, glass, and rubble) consisted of a chaotic pattern of gaping holes.

Under a Setting Sun

A bloody mess lay a few feet away. That was all that remained of Michael's body; the rest having been devoured by those wretched creatures. Simon hung his head and uttered a remorseful prayer.

All but one of the black candles had gone out. He approached the one still burning and extinguished its flame between his thumb and forefinger. It should have hurt, but he didn't feel the pain.

He staggered towards the front doors, tripping on rubble and broken pieces of candle and glass as he went. It seemed to take an age, having to dodge around the holes in the ground, but when he got there, he found that the doors weren't locked.

With a grin on his face, he threw the doors wide-open and stood, slanted, in the entrance. He sighed. There was a larger gathering of people all milling around by the gates now. That meant one final job for him before he could go home to bed. Not that sleep would come easily tonight.

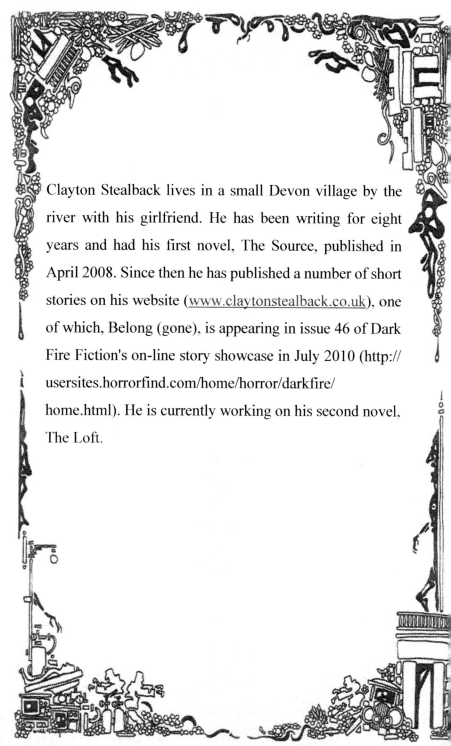

Clayton Stealback lives in a small Devon village by the river with his girlfriend. He has been writing for eight years and had his first novel, The Source, published in April 2008. Since then he has published a number of short stories on his website (www.claytonstealback.co.uk), one of which, Belong (gone), is appearing in issue 46 of Dark Fire Fiction's on-line story showcase in July 2010 (http://usersites.horrorfind.com/home/horror/darkfire/home.html). He is currently working on his second novel, The Loft.

Bury the Truth

Carole Johnstone

We most of us spend our lives frightened, though some more honestly than others. It is a fear that for the greater part is perhaps intangible, yet it follows fast on the heels of our birth and is always in the shadows; always waiting for weakness, under cover of whose wings it sneaks for-ever against us. Those shadows are greatest in the small hours of night, when self-doubt and obsession are sent to plague us.

We are all of us afraid of death. It is the human condition.

#

The third time I chose strangulation. It was far less dangerous than pills if a lot less pleasant; already my liver had been proclaimed unsalvageable by a grim-faced Resus consultant. Necessity had made self-control my only ally. Asphyxiation had become the only sensible method left to me.

I got fully dressed before feeding the scarf through the welded junction of pipes above the living room radiator. I'd downloaded detailed instructions from some God-awful website, and – should the very worst happen – I didn't want to be taken for some fetish freak whose game of solo choke-sticks had gone badly wrong. Although doubtless then that would be the least of my worries.

I tried to ignore the shaking of my hands as I wrapped the scarf around my throat, winding it round twice, breathing Alex's residual smell too deep. Already the act felt too brutal, too beyond my reserves of courage. Swallowing careful amounts of pills with pink vodka and ice had been the easier volition.

I looked at the mantelpiece and at the only photo upon it. A young couple standing in the shelter of Tower Bridge's suspended walk-way, falling snow shining brighter their smiles as skyrockets and confetti over the Thames heralded a New Year. The best year. I looked away. And tied the slip knot.

As ever, I hesitated before jumping into that abyss. As ever, I climbed down slowly, scrabbling for handholds until the way became too tangled and too sheer, escaping beyond my dominion. I let go.

My struggling ceased as I fell away from life; as the scarf tightened, biting into my throat and forcing sharp chuffs of breath from my lungs that I tried still to choke back. Storm-clouds intruded on the edges of my sight; pinwheels of bright light spun across it. The rushes of blood at my temples were mill-driven torrents of happy childhood memory. The pain was neither terrible nor exquisite. It was a malignant claustrophobia that deserved the scream I couldn't give it.

Yet the euphoria when it came was wholly unwelcome. A part of me – the admonitory voice that ever strove to be the loudest – recognised full well that this ecstasy was nothing more than hypoxia or perhaps now something far beyond it, and therefore a relief that I could hardly afford to indulge. Only the fact that it surely heralded what came next gave me the strength to both endure and ignore it.

As I searched inside myself; as I searched those choked and shadowed reaches for what I hoped and dreaded would be waiting for me, I thought again of Alex. I thought of his reckless days and tormented nights. Was this how it had been for him in the end?

Sinking ever lower, the one light in my mind dwindling almost to a pinprick, I thought not. Alex had already known what lived and waited in the very depths of this abyss. Just as They had known him.

And then something else intruded; something that I was nearly beyond remembering. The distant, shrill alarm penetrated even the roar of my starved blood – and the answer that I was now certain had almost found me. Almost. But my time was used up. I hadn't the energy to be either angry or relieved. As always, that would come later. If later came at all.

With what little strength was still mine to wield, I struck out wildly with my feet – kicking only dead air, hearing only the loose cries of gravel and scree. There might have been a very distant noise: a crash that came from the place where I had first crept down. But that place was now no more than a tiny, winking light far above my struggles.

Panic fell upon me then. Though I had no breath with which to smell, wet earth and sweet rot rushed in, filling me up, overflowing. Choking. Infecting. Soothing. The screams in my mind died. I stopped kicking.

And then – *oh blessed relief and cold terror* – there on the periphery of what little perception remained, maybe a movement. Maybe a sound. Not just one, but many. More than I had ever dreamed of. I recognised the whispered scratch of dead leaves against stone for what it truly was in the instant that Their breath was all around me.

Finally, I was in Their house.

Their laughter was almost as terrible as the skittering rush of Their feet or probe of Their fingers. Their hunger was beyond anything I had ever before imagined, even in the darkest of those dreams. In this black abyss of my own making, They found me fast in eager welcome and quicker teeth. And Their dominion was absolute. In the very instant that I celebrated my discovery, They were upon me: chuckling, biting, *dragging* my body down. Shearing careful slivers of skin from the flesh beneath, prising apart my limbs, twisting my bones, laying me bare. Piercing, licking, caressing with claws. Inflicting agonies beyond anything I had ever known. I could not see Them. These grasping little horrors. These giggling, scuttling swarms. God help me – *still* I could not see Them. Not even while they flayed me alive.

I kicked out so hard that I felt something snap inside an ankle when finally I met the wall of my prison. Hauling myself upwards in silent screams, my head beat with a tattoo that almost drowned out Their cheated fury. I crawled out of those vertiginous depths, terrorised and choking, my throat raw and eyes wet.

My hands were shaking so badly that I made do with only loosening the scarf around my neck. The living room floor was slick with urine and the air heavy with bad sweat. There was a new dent in the radiator, and the alarm clock's shrill panic rattled hard against the floorboards. I looked at the toppled crate that I had before wedged against the door, and closed my throbbing eyes. Stupid! So unbelievably stupid! That I had been conceited enough to rely upon only that.

Bury the Truth

When I had calmed down enough to move again, I switched off the alarm, hobbled to the bathroom and bound my already swollen ankle with elastic bandage. The face that looked back at me from the mirror was deathly pale, bruised sockets framing bloodshot eyes. She tried to smile, but ended up sobbing.

#

I awoke from a nightmare little more than one hour after sleep, but there was nothing unusual in that. Aside from a still throbbing ankle and a deep aching welt that reached around my throat to the angles of my jaw, there had been no after effects this time. Unless the ankle should be more than badly sprained, I would need no outside intervention at all. No drugs, no tubes, no remonstrations. Doubtless had I done, they would have listened to no more of my excuses; carting me off instead to some white-washed institution with grand walls and rattling doors.

And I had gotten further. There was no denying that. I had only panicked because I had been too close to the point of no return, and because my safety measures had been so sorely lacking.

Yet still it hadn't been enough.

As I watched reflections of rain stipple against my ceiling, I thought of Alex again.

Alex. He had always smelled of marigolds and full-tar cigarettes. His pupils tiny pinpoints overwhelmed by green, his hair too long, stubble too biting. There had been a formation of freckles on his right forearm in the shape of a five-pointed star. I remembered always thinking that these would be how I would know his corpse. But I had imagined then that such thoughts crossed the mind of anyone in love.

He had always suffered bad dreams. He had likely also uttered

209

the same whispered screams, and endured the same terrorised dread of what might be encroaching upon the space that we had shared. I had never heard him. Not until it had been too late.

Next time would be the charm. With better precautions and a stouter heart, I would see Them. I would know Them. Next time.

#

The hospital was not the one whose basement corridors had echoed my last steps toward Alex. As I followed an old couple through the automatic doors of A&E, I hardly knew whether that should make it easier or not. A trolley flanked by green suits barrelled in through a side entrance. They were already pumping saline and God knew what else into the poor bastard via intravenous drips, his heavily bandaged wrists seeping new blood.

Alex had taken pills in the end – another perverse disappointment for me, because he had been a man so driven by all that was extreme or ill-advised. He had left me a note, which had perhaps been the greater surprise. Though it had been an uninspired lament. *I want it to be over.*

Close to the obligatory anti-bacterial pumps and a large poster depicting a silhouetted nurse above the words: *It's OK to ask me if I've washed my hands*, there was an exit sign indicating the second floor. I stopped at the top of the stairs and stilled trembling fingers. Langham Ward was listed first. With only the slightest hesitation, I pushed through the swing doors.

I knew her straight away. They had put her in the bed closest to the nurses' station, and having once spent a summer as an auxiliary in Barts, I had been expecting as much. The station was the only place in the ward that would always be staffed. She was a Failed-to-Fly. The bane of any overworked shift.

She looked remarkably well for a woman who had survived suicide by train. The newspaper report had attributed her uncommon luck to a moment's indecision on the tracks, which had seen her roll into a siding seconds before impact. Instead of her life, she had lost only a leg.

"If you're another one come from upstairs, you can save your breath, love."

I stood awkwardly at the end of her bed, my thigh knocking against a bulldog clip that held pink copied charts. I belatedly wished that I'd brought some flowers as camouflage. Or a bribe.

"I don't work here, Moira."

For a moment her eyes narrowed, pulling down the swathe of bandages wrapped around her forehead. I was surprised by her age. She must have been approaching her late-forties at least. She pulled herself up against her pillows, and reached for the glasses that had been sitting in her lap. Strained layers of micropore pulled at the cannula in the back of her hand. Her first two fingers were stained dirty yellow. When I looked back at her face, she was smiling. It was a horribly vacant greeting.

"I might-a known you'd come."

I glanced at the window behind her. Though it was barely four, a few of the car park lights had already begun their night's work: emitting a dull red glow that would soon grow brighter. I imagined that I could feel their intermittent buzz under my feet.

In her grin there were more gaps than teeth. "You're younger than I'd reckoned." Under her studied south London drawl, there was still a rhotic hint of the north. Lancashire maybe. "An' you've a good share of meat on you. Cast-iron stomach is it you've still got, eh?"

When I offered no answer, her laugh was hoarse and the cough that followed it protracted. She pointed with the hand not attached to a drip. "Don't you take offence, darlin'. Don't you bloody dare. I know who you are. I know *what you do*."

A passing nurse, gowned and gloved up and carrying a contaminated waste bag, leaned close to a colleague and whispered something, sliding a glance towards us.

"Pull the curtains." Moira wasn't smiling anymore.

After shielding us from the rest of the ward in a garish, striped cocoon, I sat in the only chair. She became little more than a few tufts of wiry hair behind an orange-painted bedside table. There were no cards on that table, no flowers.

"Get over here."

She didn't take up much of the bed. When I perched beside her, we remained still far apart. The smell of her sweat was sickly sweet. I noticed the silver lines that ran alongside the bruised veins of her wrists like B-roads on a map. When she saw me looking, she snatched down her gown's sleeves, shooting me a gaze so venomous – so violated – that I dropped my own to the floor.

"Who was you to him, darlin', eh? His girlfriend?" A tongue coated in white flicked out over her teeth in a lascivious grin. "His Friday night winch?"

Still I didn't answer. None of the others had been like this. They had been defeated, angry, suspicious even. But they'd all been afraid too. And every one of them had wanted to talk. In the end.

Bury the Truth

"We're not stupid, love. An' we keep after our own. Them posts kept on comin' even after Alex was back in't ground." She suddenly caught herself short, and reached for the plastic cup on her bedside table. Her hands were shaking as she tipped it back. A tiny rivulet escaped her mouth, running down her chin before staining dark the neck of her gown.

"I found the link in Alex's inbox. When he died, I had to–"

She wafted a vague hand towards me, as if the woes of those left behind were less than inconsequential. When she spoke again, all trace of Lancashire had gone.

"Alex was a *green-skite*. D'you know what that means, darlin'? He trusted folks with things they'd no business knowin'. You're likely jus' the only one who believed him."

I found myself drawn to the raised outline of Moira's right leg, and alongside it the flat expanse of sheet that used to be her left. I imagined its incineration in some basement furnace – and then remembered the stink of Alex's scarf as it had burned to ash in the kitchen sink. It wasn't healthy for me to be here, it was the very opposite of that. And yet I kept on coming. Different faces, different wards. Same old reason.

Moira squirmed a little in her swaddle of sheets. "And just what did the *green-skite* tell you?"

"All of it."

Moira's eyes grew sharp, and her breath whistled through pursed lips. "Don't be cute, darlin'." For a horrible moment she reminded me of my mother. "He tell you 'bout them little beasties?"

When she saw me flinch; when she realised that she'd got one over on me, her perpetual smile grew teeth again. "Oh aye, I kenned tha knew about the wee hungry bastards that are waitin' for their chow. Waitin' in the dark. Waitin' in the death."

A memory so vivid that it almost wrenched a scream from my throat saw me retreat from the bed too fast. I remembered the feel of Them on my flesh. The little nips of Their teeth, the tear of Their eager fingers. I remembered a dread anticipation that was almost sexual: *la petite mort* of an ecstasy so intense it was nothing but pain. And I remembered the dark – the scuttling, suffocating dark – and the unending end that crouched inside it.

"Aubrey told me you was askin'." Moira's voice had calmed, recovering its careful drawl.

When I looked again, her eyes were no longer as bright. The uncertain question in them was worse.

"He says to me: 'Alex's girl came by that first night they brought me in'. Think he was even a bit pleased – old fool."

"I just want to know, Moira. I just want to understand."

"He finally did it, you know. Done himself in last Monday week." She ignored my hissed intake of breath. "Oh, we're not much fuckin' use to you then, are we, love? Just one more for the wee bastards' table."

"I didn't–"

Moira stabbed a long, yellow-stained nail at her chest, hard enough to leave purple moon-shaped welts. "*I'll* not be helpin' tha though. I'll not be satisfying any sick little car-wreck-gawping bitch's curiosity." Her final jab broke through the skin, and she snatched her hand back with a curse.

I didn't answer her. She was wrong, but I knew she'd never believe it. It wasn't fascination that drove me to seek out those like Alex:

those he had confided in, those who had shared his terrible burden. It was fear – the very worst kind. The kind that was an itch deep down to the bone. The kind that would never let me forget, never let me rest. Not until I knew it all. Not until I'd seen Them for real.

"You look like Daddy got you into the best grammar school, the fanciest university." The thin river of blood that ran the gauntlet of rib protrusions before disappearing into the shadow of her breastbone belied her smirk. "Ever read the Divine Comedy, darlin'?"

I might have looked shocked – and not just because of the abrupt change in subject – because some measure of shine came back into her eyes. "Oh aye, it might look like there's not much rattlin' about up here. But when you know what I know, you look for answers."

I ventured back towards the bed. It had sounded almost like an invitation.

"Everyone hates the Suicides, love. *Everyone*." She leaned closer. "The Suicides get sent to the seventh ring – seventh of nine – seems a wee bit over the top when all's that we're ever hurtin' is ourselves, eh?"

I tried to hold her gaze, even when she wiped the blood from her chest onto the sheet before dropping it over my hands. She leaned closer still. "Do you know where they'd send you? They'd send you to the last *bolgia* in the Eighth Circle, darlin'. They'd bury tha so deep in the Inferno, your fucking piss would boil black."

I slapped her without thinking – and I did it hard enough to hurt my own hand. "What is *wrong* with you?" This had never happened before. This had never even come close to happening before.

"You know what's wrong with me, love." Those mean pinheads still shone in her eyes, but the hand that cradled the cheek I'd slapped

215

had begun its trembling again. "I'm cursed. Just like Aubrey, just like Alex. *Nothin'* like you."

"You don't think I'm cursed?"

"No! You was born of life – not death. Your mother cried you to her breast as *our* mothers grew cold and let in Their whispers to poison us. You are nothin' but a stupid wee lassie who fell in love with an abomination."

"How can you call him that?" Alex: beautiful, cursed Alex, whose dreams had stolen between us like a terrible thief. "You're the same! You're–"

"A drunken squaddie stole my mother's life, darlin'. The blood wasn't even dry when they pulled me out of her. *Your* Alex wriggled his way out of a dead and buried corpse." She relinquished her hold on me with a triumphant flourish. "*That* is an abomination."

I got an unwelcome flash of the headline that Alex had eventually shown me: an old newspaper print that he had kept hidden in the drawer under his bed. Only two words – but two words put down in a black-blocked scream. *Grave Baby.*

"Time for your medication, Moira."

I jumped guiltily up from the bed when the nurse entered. She barely looked in my direction at all.

"No."

"Just bloody take it." Tired apathy was replaced by a hard-edged fury that the nurse might have better disguised had the curtain not shielded her from the rest of the ward. "And keep the noise down." She turned her glare onto me. "Or you'll have to leave. Capiche?"

Bury the Truth

I swallowed down the sudden urge to laugh, and nodded instead.

After the nurse had left, Moira spat out the pain pill and pushed it under her pillow. She sighed long and low. "If I tell you what you want to hear will you leave me be?"

"Yes."

"You want to know what it's like bein' me? You want to hear about the worm that's wrapped round my brain; the things it whispers to me every day and every night?"

I didn't know. All of a sudden I didn't know why I was there at all.

Her chuckle was joyless. The light had gone out of her eyes. "I had my first dream when I was three years old."

I bit down on my incredulity, though I think she saw it well enough.

"Them little monsters crept into my empty dreams and whispered in my ear. They told me They was hungry. That They was always hungry and always havin' to wait. Their wee fuckin' teeth and *claws* have stripped me to the bone every night since – and every one of them suffered is a night closer to Them gettin' me back for real."

She coughed once and then twice, a spasm wracking her bony frame. "They want us all back, darlin', but you already ken that, don't tha? They give us our life for such a short time – and then They snatch us back into the abyss."

There was something horribly childlike in her sudden smile. Something very close to insanity. "But They like *us* the best – us with the dead mothers and the worms in our brains. Us cursed with the knowin' of where we all came from. And where we all go back to. An' your Alex They're still takin' Their time over, I don't doubt. Savourin' every last morsel."

I fell back against nothing then. Fighting dead space, I scrabbled for a hold on the striped curtain – and it reminded me so suddenly of my falling into that same dreadful abyss, Alex's scarf wrapped tight around my throat, that I almost screamed.

Moira made to get out of the bed as if to help me before sinking back against her damp pillows. "All of us cursed ones end up doin' ourselves in sooner or later."

"Why?" I was still on the floor, my fists wound tight around the curtain. "Why, for Christ's sake would you *choose* to go back?"

Moira gave a coquettish shrug. "Why do people do themselves in before the cancer can? It's not the pain they're scared of. It's the dyin'." This time her smile was almost serene. "But they do it anyways."

"Moira–"

"Oh, you think you're so special, is it, love? You thinks kennin' is the same as seein'. As *feelin'*." Those pinheads flashed back so quick and so wide that I flinched. The swaying curtain tickled my neck. "It's not. No, Mam, it's fuckin' not."

"Why am I so terrible, Moira? I only want to understand why–"

"Because tha was blessed!" She tore the sheets from her body, exposing her stump and the blood that had seeped onto the mattress beneath. Her entire body trembled, her catheter bag wobbling precari- ously on the lowered guardrail. "You was blessed with the not knowin' –

and yet you seeked the darkness out. You threw away what life gave you! What it could never give to us!"

When I tried to reach out to her, she flinched away, dragging her ruined leg backward in a dark smeared trail. The plastic frame of her catheter bag finally fell away from the bed and slapped hard against the floor. That finger shook in my direction again.

She had been the one that I'd been trying to find ever since Alex's death had left me adrift. Even as Moira condemned my endless search in spitting derision, she gave to me my every answer. My every suspicion. Clearly this showed too readily upon my face, because her own grew even wilder. The stench of her spilled urine filled our false isolation in a bitter, pungent shout.

"I don't know what Alex seen. I know he seen worse than me because I read his posts. But I can't *know*. Not the same as he did." Her eyes narrowed again. "You, my precious darlin', are *so terrible,* because you think a frightened whisper in the dark is no different to seein' those beady little eyes, feelin' your insides torn out and danced over with skittered feet, knowin' that this is death and forever. Forever and never nothin' else again."

"I know."

Her laugh was brittle, eyes dull – but I saw the awful curiosity there too. It was quiet and it was disbelieving. But it was there.

"I know, Moira. Maybe not as much as you, maybe you're right about that. But I do know. I *know.*"

"How many times?" Her voice was a dead, dragged weight.

I paused only for a moment. "Three."

The tears fell over the hand pressed to her mouth. They soaked into the micropore that had bunched and peeled away from the needle at her wrist. "Oh, you stupid, stupid child."

"See? I've seen Their abyss, I've *seen* it. I'm just like you." My lips had stuck against my teeth, and my tongue was too dry to come to their aid. My voice came out as a pleading whisper. "I'm just like Alex."

She reached for me then, pulling me against her cold, damp, bony body with a murmured cry. "No, lassie."

When she stroked my hair back from my face, she reminded me so terribly of my mother that I could hardly breathe for my own sobs. My mother was already with Them.

After a few minutes Moira drew away, and when I looked into her eyes, those pinheads still shone behind the tears, the hopelessness. The ugly pity.

"You invite death to see it, darlin'," she whispered. "We welcome an end to sufferin' its dread." She tried to grab for me but I had already shrunk from her grasp. "That can never be the same. Not ever."

#

I sat with her for maybe another hour that night. She slept for a time and suffered no ill dreams as far as I could tell, but it was a fitful slumber only lightly endured. At around ten, I made to leave, although I was loath to do it. Despite her rancour and the dead shine in her eyes, Moira was everything I had left.

I only asked her one more question, and it was one that she met with an easier, kinder smile.

"Why couldn't you do it?"

"Because the flesh is weak, darlin'." Her gaze was horribly beseeching – all the more so because we both knew I wouldn't listen.

220

Bury the Truth

"Choose the *straight way*, lassie. You'll find the *basso loco* where the sun is silent soon enough. We all do."

"Why couldn't you do it, Moira?"

Her crooked teeth disappeared for the last time. She pressed down the fraying tape at her wrist and wouldn't look back at me again. "Because I'm frightened. *I'm frightened to death*. Always have been."

But I knew she would. As I waited outside for the last shuttle bus home, the hospital a stark, bright square against the dull exhale of the city behind, I remembered the envious look in her eyes when she had talked of Aubrey's final success. I whispered the very last words she'd spoken to me before I pulled that striped curtain between us.

"Dante might have been wrong about there bein' a final judgement or any kind of paradise, but time *does* end. In the House of Death, everyone knows and remembers nothin'. An' that's no punishment, love. That's bliss."

I knew that she would do it.

#

That night I picked at a take away chow mein and watched the Eastenders omnibus. I phoned my father while sifting through old photographs of Alex and I, in what I had before imagined were happier times. The rain started up again around nine, and I closed the curtains against both it and the interminable thrum of the streetlights outside.

I had tied the noose around the only surviving rafter in the hall. Its melodramatic shadow might otherwise have dissuaded me. Only once I was truly ready did I venture out onto the landing. I didn't write a note. The only person to whom I might have written one had already gone.

As I wobbled on the three-legged stool and drew the rope over my still bruised throat, I remembered the touch of Their fingers and the snap of Their teeth. I remembered the eager clamour of Their hunger and those childlike squalls of glee. I remembered the smell of rot and earth washing away the clean, hot screams of my flesh. All that I was.

And I remembered the only line from the Divine Comedy that I'd ever known. *Abandon all hope, ye who enter here*. After everything, it had been all that I'd ever needed to know at all.

As I pushed away the stool, I went kicking and screaming with the best of them. Into the abyss. Into Their house: the ones that ever wanted us back. Perhaps Alex yet waited for me there.

The fourth time was the charm.

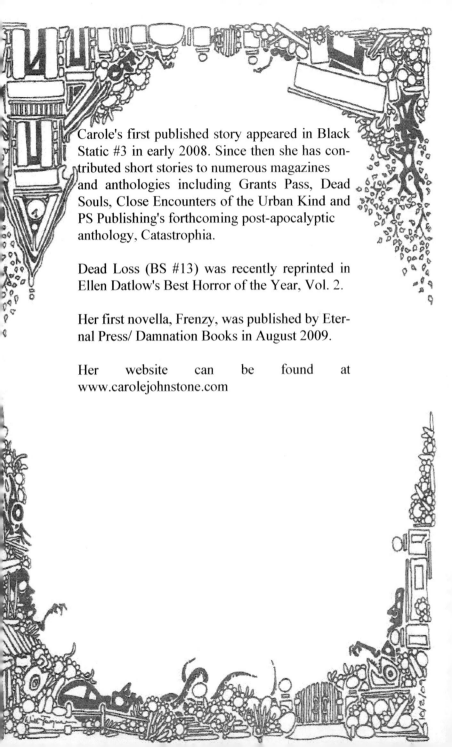

Carole's first published story appeared in Black Static #3 in early 2008. Since then she has contributed short stories to numerous magazines and anthologies including Grants Pass, Dead Souls, Close Encounters of the Urban Kind and PS Publishing's forthcoming post-apocalyptic anthology, Catastrophia.

Dead Loss (BS #13) was recently reprinted in Ellen Datlow's Best Horror of the Year, Vol. 2.

Her first novella, Frenzy, was published by Eternal Press/ Damnation Books in August 2009.

Her website can be found at www.carolejohnstone.com

Vincent Chong is an award-winning freelance illustrator and designer. Currently living and working in the UK, his art and design has been published internationally and can be seen on book covers, magazines, CD packaging and websites. He has worked for clients around the world including HarperCollins and Little, Brown and has illustrated the works of authors such as Ray Bradbury and Stephen King. Vincent has received the British Fantasy Award for 'Best Artist' three years running in 2007, 2008 and 2009. You can learn more about Vincent at his website, www.vincentchong-art.co.uk and blog, vincentchongart.wordpress.com.

Will Jacques is a product of the hippie culture of Boulder Colorado circa 1978. Early in his childhood, he developed an unnatural interest in all things spooky. Since then, he has amassed a huge collection of supernatural fiction.

Jacques is a traditional pen-and-ink artist. He draws freehand with a Uniball pen without any hint of a plan or formula. Jacques never uses a pencil, a strait-edge, or any form of technology.

When not drawing, Jacques enjoys playing the mandola, juggling, riding the unicycle, reading dark tomes of forgotten lore, hunting ghosts, and teaching middle school science.

Jacques currently divides his time between Montana, and South Georgia. He is married with two kids and two dogs.